Keela had never seen her daughter smile so much.

Every time she watched "Doctor Dan" with Anna, Keela's heart warmed and her thoughts wandered to a secret and special place.

Suddenly, he got serious and turned to Anna. "Maybe it's time you dropped the doctor part and just call me Dan?" He glanced at Keela, as if to get her approval about letting Anna call him that. She nodded.

Hugging the stuffed otter Daniel had bought her at the aquarium, Anna grinned. "I'm going to name him Dan."

"Wow, you're naming a toy after me? I've finally arrived."

Anna hugged Daniel. The real one. "Because I love you."

The room went momentarily silent. Stunned into silence was more like it. Keela could see Daniel struggling with how to respond to such a spontaneous declaration. Where she wasn't ready to say the word, her daughter fearlessly exclaimed it. Love! Clearly it rattled him—it rattled her, too—and he wasn't sure what to say or do.

After a pause, with a serious and kind expression on his face, Daniel reached for Anna's shoulder. "You know what, Anna-bug, I love you, too."

* * *

THE DELANEYS OF SANDPIPER BEACH:
A family business with room to grow...

Dear Reader,

I'm so happy to share my twenty-fifth Harlequin book, *Forever a Father*, the launch book for The Delaneys of Sandpiper Beach trilogy. In book one, I introduce Daniel Delaney, the eldest brother, and Keela O'Mara, a young lady from Ireland who works for him. The more I got to know Daniel and Keela, the more I rooted for them and their happily-ever-after. If any couple deserved it, they did, but both had been disillusioned by love and have the emotional scars to prove it.

As Keela's boss, Daniel is aware he walks a fine line if he lets his attraction to his employee get out of hand. He's starting a new business, and he needs her expertise to keep things running smoothly. That should be all. Enter Keela's four-year-old daughter, Anna, and Daniel's eighty-five-year-old grandfather, Padraig, and things really get complicated. With the beautiful Sandpiper Beach as a backdrop, and a prediction from a fortune cookie, Daniel and Keela begin to tiptoe toward the *L* word, and in so doing, help each other conquer their heartache.

Now settle in and meet the family: Padraig, Maureen (Mom), Sean (Dad) and brothers Daniel, Mark and Conor. The Delaneys may run the third-best hotel in Sandpiper Beach, but where family, love and loyalty are concerned, they're hands-down number one.

And if you didn't know, I love hearing from readers! Go to www.lynnemarshall.com, where you can sign up for an occasional newsletter and keep up with all the latest info and contests.

Thanks for reading,

Lynne

Forever a Father

Lynne Marshall

ISBN-13: 978-1-335-46564-1

Forever a Father

This edition published by arrangement with Harlequin Books S.A.

For questions and comments about the quality of this book, please contact us at CustomerService@Harlequin.com.

Printed in U.S.A.

Lynne Marshall used to worry she had a serious problem with daydreaming, and then she discovered she was supposed to write those stories down! A late bloomer, she came to fiction writing after her children were nearly grown. Now she battles the empty nest by writing romantic stories about life, love and happy endings. She's a proud mother and grandmother who loves babies, dogs, books, music and traveling.

Books by Lynne Marshall

Harlequin Special Edition

Her Perfect Proposal
A Doctor for Keeps
The Medic's Homecoming
Courting His Favorite Nurse

Harlequin Medical Romance

Miracle for the Neurosurgeon
A Mother for His Adopted Son
200 Harley Street: American Surgeon in London
Her Baby's Secret Father

Summer Brides

Wedding Date with the Army Doc

The Hollywood Hills Clinic

His Pregnant Sleeping Beauty

Cowboys, Doctors...Daddies!

Hot-Shot Doc, Secret Dad
Father for Her Newborn Baby

Visit the Author Profile page at Harlequin.com for more titles.

Sincerest thanks to Flo Nicoll for guiding me
through the early stages of this project.
To Gail Chasan for giving me the chance to tell the
Delaney brothers' stories for Special Edition.
And special thanks to Megan Broderick
for stepping up on my behalf.
I am deeply grateful.

Chapter One

Daniel Delaney opened the clinic supply closet, but it was nearly bare. "Keela!" He called for his physical therapy assistant before filtering the frustration out of his voice. What was going on? She was usually on top of everything related to the job, yet here he stood, with not a single Velcro tendonitis strap in sight. Disappointed, he glanced around. Where were the red stretch bands, or the electrical pads for the TENS machine? Eyes darting every which way, he added several other items to the list. "Keela!"

The PT in question stuck her head into the tiny supply closet, her large baby blues registering alarm. "Yes?"

"Where is everything?" He glanced around to emphasize the point.

Her light brown brows lowered and she stepped inside. "I told you last week the weather conditions in the

East had set back the delivery dates on my last order." Unlike him, she spoke civilly, though she folded her thin arms and lifted her slightly squared chin.

"You did?" He'd worked with her for three months, had hired her on the spot the day she'd walked in, which was unlike him. But after having lost on short notice his first PT tech, Tiffany, he needed a replacement. He'd also been limping through an ongoing private hell, making him a bear to work with, which was probably why Tiffany had quit in the first place. That and his high expectations for his employees. Like expecting them to be on time. Bullheaded to a fault, he'd attempted to do everything himself for one long, stressful month and failed miserably. Chalking that up as a major blunder, he'd accepted his shortcoming. He'd been a guy who'd gotten too full of himself with opening his own physical medicine practice, and who'd thought he could do it all…while grieving. Lesson learned.

On the other hand, he'd had a hunch about the woman from Ireland who'd just completed her accredited associate degree from the local city college, and who desperately needed the job. Maybe the accent he recognized in his own grandfather swayed him a teeny tiny bit. She was new in town, divorced, and had a child to support, and was the complete opposite of Tiffany, who'd complained he was too demanding when he insisted she show up for work on time and finish everything before she left. Keela was employee-of-the-month material.

He hadn't regretted spontaneously hiring her, either. She was particularly good at dealing with his no-longer-sunny personality and letting his occasional gruffness roll off her skin. Like right now, when he wasn't ready to admit she may have told him this information before. "Hmm."

"I should know never to talk to you when you've got your head buried in paperwork." She gave an understanding smile, the kind that always brightened her eyes and disarmed him.

"So when's the order expected?" Standing nearly nose to nose with her in the tight chamber felt cramped. Plus her vanilla herb perfume was disturbing; he didn't know whether to sniff her or nibble her neck, which for some reason made him cranky again. He motioned for her to back out, she did and he followed.

"They promised before the end of this week."

He let out his breath. "Then I guess we'll just have to make do."

Her sometimes distracting smile stretched wider. "That's what you said last time." She turned in the short hallway, the *gotcha* moment causing a nearly imperceptible twitch of one brow, and went back into the physical therapy room, where the first of her afternoon patients waited.

Point taken, and true, he let his job preoccupy him. A perfect excuse to push his ongoing grief aside. The clinic was his bread and butter, and lately there'd been more crust than bread, and only a thin layer of no-name buttery spread. But he was determined to make the business side of medicine work right here in his hometown, Sandpiper Beach. Even though beach towns were notoriously tough on new businesses, and moving back home after losing the woman you loved wasn't the best reason to throw yourself into a new business venture. But he did love his job.

He'd wanted to become a physical medicine doctor since he was an injured preteen jock and had been sent to one for multiple issues, all of which related to overdoing it in sports. The doctor had worked wonders on his aches and pains without loading him up on pills, handing him back his jock status to play football and baseball to his heart's content. Daniel quickly became a believer. In fact, it changed his life. From that point forward he'd set his goal on the prize of medicine. The refocus may also have had something to do with the reality check that he wasn't big or burly enough for professional sports. Whatever the true reason, he'd worked tirelessly throughout high school, college, medical school and his residency/fellowship. For this. He glanced around the small, functional clinic as he walked back to his office, the pride planted in his chest blooming a bit. He'd actually done it—survived the first year without Kathryn *and* in business.

Business ran in the family. Padraig Delaney, his eighty-five-year-old grandfather, had immigrated to the United States in the 1950s, where he helped develop the lush golf courses along the central California coast. There he'd met Mary and made her his wife. They'd scrimped and saved and bought property in Sandpiper Beach because it reminded him of Sligo Bay way back home in County Sligo, Ireland. Soon after, he and Mary built a small beachside hotel and called it The Drumcliffe.

Daniel's father had taken over what was now a family business, after giving up teaching at the local high school, and Daniel's mother managed reservations and hospitality. Dad had taken to the new job happily and likewise encouraged Daniel to work for himself. He'd been perfectly content with a good job in a hospital group down in Ventura, California, but within a year his personal life had taken a hit. Kathryn had left him. After the major setback, he'd fallen into such a slump that he decided to move back to his beach hometown and set up practice right here. He loved his parents and liked hanging out with his brothers, and Sandpiper Beach would always be home. With or without Kathryn.

The clinic soon became his sole focus, and with grief and pain as his constant companions, Daniel was convinced this business had saved his life.

He scratched out a note on his prescription pad: "One Velcro tendonitis strap." Then he stepped back into the patient exam room. "John, sorry to inconvenience you, but you'll have to get this filled at the local pharmacy. We're currently out of stock."

The middle-aged man suffering from new-onset tennis elbow took the script and thanked him. "No problem."

"If you have any questions about how to put it on, come on in and either I or Keela will show you." He demonstrated where on the forearm to place an imaginary strap and how to attach it without cutting off the circulation. "It's not a tourniquet. Oh, and you can keep taking the over-the-counter anti-inflammatories, but don't forget to use ice, too. If in a couple of weeks you're not making any progress, we could try a wrist extensor, or after a month or so give you an injection, but let's start with this."

"Will do, Doc." The silver-templed man hopped off the exam table. "Still feels strange to call little Danny Delaney 'Doc.'" He winked a blue eye and shook Daniel's hand, then winced from the tendonitis pain. "Thanks for being here. Otherwise I'd have had to drive forty miles for help."

"Glad to be here, John. We'll get this worked out even if I have to bring you in for some low level laser therapy."

He escorted the patient to the hallway and, after

watching him exit to the reception area, pivoted toward his small corner office to push through more paperwork before his next appointment in—he glanced at his watch—ten minutes.

"Daniel?" Keela popped out of the therapy room.

He glanced up, momentarily content being the guy in charge.

She approached, looking far better in their khaki cargo pants and white polo shirt uniform than he did. "You've written ten repetitions ten times a day for this." She pointed to the exercise regimen he'd created especially for the patient. "Sure you didn't mean three times a day?"

Were the unwanted thoughts from when he woke up this morning, about Kathryn and everything they'd lost, going to set the tone for yet another day? He gave his screwup face and, without saying a word, took the paper and made the correction, which got another one of those beyond-pleasant grins from his PT assistant. Yup, he noticed. Again.

Keela O'Mara cracked a smile at her boss's silly face. He'd crossed his forest-green eyes and tipped his oblong chin, just like her four-year-old daughter sometimes did when she colored outside the lines. Sure, he was often gruff, but she didn't take it personally. On the contrary, she trusted him for it, knowing what she saw was what she'd get. The guy was honest with his reactions, and she could deal with that. There was no question this clinic meant everything to him.

She liked working for Daniel Delaney and had hit the jackpot when she'd landed this job right out of Central Coast City College. Many of her classmates were still scrambling for work nearly four months later. Being back in Sandpiper Beach was a blessing after struggling for the last year and a half since the divorce from Ron.

Six years ago she'd started an online friendship with a guy in California. Living in Ennis, County Clare, Ireland, she'd thought the whole thing rather daring, yet safe. He liked her being from Ireland, and after six months she'd agreed to meet him for coffee on his layover at Shannon Airport.

His big brown eyes and warm, wide smile won her over immediately, then he proved to be the perfect gentleman. She'd known her share of smooth talkers, but this guy was polite and polished, and she wanted to know him better. When she'd wished out loud that she could show him around Ennis, he'd magically arranged to cut his vacation in Europe short by a few days to see her again. Her parents even liked him!

One thing led to another and he'd offered to fly her to California for a visit. Her parents cautioned her, so she'd made a firm request: *I can't stay with you, Ron.* But he'd already booked her a room in a small hotel by the beach, The Drumcliffe—the people who owned and operated it were Irish Americans, he'd said, to make her feel at home—then he'd proved to be the perfect gentleman the whole visit. That was when she fell in love.

She'd been working as a massage therapist at a day spa in Ennis, getting by on her tips, but not earning enough to move away from home, let alone plan another trip to California. Two months later, she'd discovered she'd fallen pregnant. And though eventually Ron had asked her to marry him, he never seemed quite the same sweet-talking guy again.

Ten after four on Wednesday afternoon, Keela came strolling out of the therapy room. As she and her patient emerged from the hallway, Daniel was at the copier, collating packets for the athletic department staff at Central Coast City College—otherwise known as the 4Cs—for the upcoming presentation he had planned for tomorrow morning. Keela accompanied Mrs. Joan Haverhill, a long-term client at the Delaney Physical Medicine Clinic. That was, if you counted "long-term" as the one year since he'd opened his business.

"With your joints being fine, and considering normal wear and tear…" Keela said to the patient while nodding to acknowledge Daniel.

"Go ahead, say it—*for a woman my age*," the tall, yet hunch-shouldered, gray-haired woman complained. "It's all I ever hear when I go to the doctor these days. *For your age.*" She made sure Daniel heard her, too.

A lyrical laugh eased out of Keela's mouth, and it never failed to grab his attention. She might as well be singing.

"I'd never say that, Mrs. Haverhill. You're in great shape—"

The sixtyish lady tossed Daniel a deadpan look that seemed to say, *Do you believe the crock she's feeding me? More, please.*

He smiled and added a benevolent nod.

"For your age," Joan repeated, first pasting her gaze on him, then slowly looking back to Keela. "Kind of like the old joke about fortune cookies."

Keela gave a blank stare. Joan glanced toward Daniel again. "Dr. Delaney, you've got to take your employees for Chinese food once in a while."

The woman turned her attention back to Keela. "Here's the old trick—all you have to do is add 'in bed' to whatever the fortune says." Keela canted her head, considering Joan's suggestion. "Um, let me think… For example, 'Do not mistake temptation for opportunity,' then you add 'in bed.' Get it? It always works, just add 'in bed.'"

For her effort, Joan received another uncertain stare. "Didn't you ever do that, Dr. Delaney?"

He pressed his lips together and slowly shook his head. "Can't say I ever have."

Resigned, she shrugged. "Maybe that was only my generation. Anyway, that's the way it seems these days. Every doctor report I get either begins or ends with the phrase *for your a*—"

"In bed?" Keela teased.

Mrs. Haverhill gave an uncharacteristic chuckle. And that was another thing he liked about his employee. She was quick-witted.

"In that case, I want you to do these four exercises I've just shown you, three times a day..." Keela gestured for Joan to finish the sentence.

"...in bed." The lady winked at Daniel.

"Yes. Well, *on* a bed, actually. Or better yet, on this mat." Keela breezed to the cubicles that lined the hallway, which thankfully weren't depleted like the supply shelves, and grabbed a bright pink yoga mat.

Having clearly won over the usually reticent client with the parting gift—another touch Daniel was proud to offer his patients but was worried he'd have to give up if business didn't pick up soon—Keela received a smile from Mrs. Haverhill, who took the mat and headed for the door to the waiting room. "Thank you."

"Have a great week!"

"In bed or for a woman my age?" Joan snickered as she went out.

Keela stood watching the client leave for a moment, then turned toward Daniel with a satisfied smile.

How could he not smile back? "Good work."

As assistant physical therapists went, Daniel had known from the start she was damn good. It was the rest of the package that made him uncomfortable. The woman part.

Especially after Kathryn, who'd been responsible for his deciding to come back home. He'd asked her to move to Sandpiper Beach with him, so they could heal together. Instead she'd left, essentially gutting him.

"Thanks, boss." Keela saluted and gathered the batch of paperwork for the next appointment. He'd asked her to see a few extra clients this afternoon so he could concentrate on his pitch for tomorrow. If he could land the 4Cs account, he'd be sitting pretty, with a never-ending flow of young athletes through his office doors. He needed to get it right.

Keela's phone rang and she stepped inside her office to answer it. With the copier going, Daniel couldn't hear the conversation, but as he gazed through the large office window, he noticed her brows were lowered. She said something else, then glanced toward the ceiling in a frustrated manner while listening. Just as his copies were done, she hung up, her shoulders slumped and her usual smile inverted. "Thanks for the too-late heads-up," she raised her voice to the phone on her desk.

No sooner had she stepped into the hallway than a little girl barreled through the doorway from reception, an older woman at her heels. Keela's face lit up when she saw the child. "Hi, Anna," she sang, bending and giving her a hug.

Up until now Daniel had just seen pictures of Keela's daughter on her desk. That, he could handle, but seeing her in person sent a painful jolt straight through his chest. He flinched, then quickly got a grip, though thanks to his recent history, looking at her felt like slowing down at a car accident. Man, she was small, with the kind of little-kid smile that belonged on a billboard. A junior version of her mother's. He diverted his gaze to the paperwork in his hands.

"Thanks for dropping by on your way to your appointment, Mrs. Jenkins." Acting upbeat seemed to be second nature to Keela, but this time it didn't ring true.

Daniel stacked his handouts in a huge pile and started for his office, and shortly afterward the woman left, leaving Anna behind. He tried not to notice.

He'd just plopped the copies on his desk when he felt someone behind him. Keela stood at his office entrance, an anxious expression on her face, her daughter at her side. "I need to ask you a huge favor," she said. "My ex-husband was supposed to take Anna for the afternoon and evening, but he only just now called and canceled, and Mrs. Jenkins has an appointment to get her hair colored."

Daniel dreaded what he suspected was coming. His usual, nearly daily struggle with his loss had lightened up lately, thanks to the distraction of responsibilities with the clinic, but the mere sight of the impish little girl managed to decimate in a few seconds what progress he'd made over the past year. Slipping into defense mode, he went practical.

"You can leave her in your office if you need to."

"Uh, no, she's only four."

"I'm almost five." The child's tiny hand shot up, all five fingers worth, which clawed at his achy heart. He had to admit the kid was cute, with loads of curls and big brown eyes, but…

"She needs supervision."

No. No. No. Not a good day for this. "Do you want to

cancel your afternoon appointments? It's kind of late."

Keep thinking about the business. That, I can handle. But if he took over her schedule, he wouldn't have the time he'd allotted to practice his pitch for tomorrow.

"No!" Alarm made Keela's large iceberg-blue eyes grow huge. "I wouldn't leave you in a bind like that. I've got four more patients to see, and I intend to see them." She chewed her lip, her daughter holding her hand and staring up at her. The innocent party. "Is there any chance you could look after her for the next hour?"

What? I've got things to do. Presentations to prepare for. I don't do *kids.* But he wasn't that big of a jerk, was he? Keela was his employee of the month, every month. Hell, every day! She needed a favor, and he was it. "I guess she can sit in here while I work." He didn't even try to sound okay with the idea, and put the emphasis on *work*, as tension crept up his neck.

"Thank you!" she said, with such relief that he felt bad for his contrary attitude, even as early signs of panic set in. But he had a presentation to prepare for! He would just ignore the kid and soon the hour would be over.

"Let's not make a habit of it." The thought of spending forced time with the little girl sent an ice pick straight through his heart. Would he ever get beyond it?

"Never my intention, Daniel. I'm just stuck in the middle today."

He clenched his molars. Yeah, he got that. Now he was, too, but childcare wasn't part of their employment agreement. He had a business to run. It was his lifeline. "Okay, kid, have a seat."

The little girl looked to her mother, who dropped to her knees and gazed at her, eye to eye. "Be a good girl for Dr. Delaney. Mommy needs to work, okay?"

Anna nodded, as serious as a little kid could be. Keela took the tiny, tangerine-colored backpack covered in animated movie characters off the child's shoulders, unzipped it and fished out some crayons and a coloring book. "You can make some nice pictures for Daddy for when you see him next." Then she escorted the girl to the chair opposite Daniel's desk. The one he reserved for his patients. There was a small table with assorted magazines next to it. She could color on that. She was so tiny, and probably worried about the big mean-faced man. He tried to smile to ease her concerns, but failed. It wasn't her fault she'd been stuck with him, old mean-face, who was still hurting and lost and, so far, unable to move on.

Anna didn't seem too interested in drawing for her dad, but Keela opened the book to a specific page. She left for the therapy room on a wave of that vanilla herb scent, with a relived "thank you" on her breath, and thankfully, the child went right to work on her coloring.

Okay, so far so good. He'd survive, he'd get through this, and before he knew it, the time would be over. *Think defense.* He checked his watch, then got back to the task at hand, ignoring the kid.

"What are you doing?" The slow, inquisitive words broke his concentration. He tensed. Again.

"Uh, I'm working on a project."

"Can I help?"

He stapled pages together from the large stack waiting on his desk. Daniel wanted to breeze through the mindless job in record time so he could practice his presentation until he knew it backward and forward. But there she was, standing next to his desk. He stopped and glanced at the kid, noting her hopeful dark eyes, her obvious eagerness to get involved. Man, ignoring her was tough. "Uh, okay. Can you push this down hard enough to go through the papers?"

He placed the stapler at the upper left corner of the next four-page packet on his desk. She was too short to reach it, so he held the stapler out to her, trying to keep some distance. Not the right angle, and zero support. She climbed up on his lap, and he instantly regretted it. How tiny she was, yet full of life, how…

Bang, she whopped that stapler like a professional, surprising him. "Good." If they worked fast, this would soon be over.

A minute later she'd completed the task, with his guidance, and somehow he'd survived. "And that's it. Thanks. Now you can go back to your coloring." He immediately removed the child from his lap, finally able to relax and take a deep breath.

It occurred to him he might stick Abby, the receptionist, with Anna for a while. But Keela had asked him to do the job, and he'd already assigned Abby to update client records this afternoon, which involved calling former and current patients on the phone. Otherwise known as drumming up more business. She couldn't very well do that, check in the arriving patients and watch a kid, too. And he'd cleared most of his afternoon specifically so he could work on his 4Cs pitch for tomorrow morning.

"I don't want to."

"What?"

"I don't want to color. Is that a fountain?"

Looking out the door, she said the word slowly—*"foun-tan."* Yes, it was. It was in the hallway and she was welcome to go get a drink so he could get back to what he needed to do. "Yes. Help yourself."

Anna scooted out of the room in her pink leggings

and tutu, her sneakers squeaking on the tile. It was kind of cute, but he ignored the thought. Too damn painful. Instead he gave a sigh of relief that he was alone again and focused on his speech.

"I need help!" She used her outdoor voice, which startled him, and he jumped out of his chair to assist her by lifting her under the arms. Man, she was light, hardly weighed anything. So vulnerable and completely dependent on him. So trusting. Precious. She pushed the button for water, but her mop of curls got in the way. Her face got wet and she giggled. He almost smiled.

"Here," he said, balancing her on his bent knee and thigh, and holding her hair out of the way with one hand. She slurped to her heart's content, coming up only when she needed to breathe.

"Tastes good."

He thought quickly. "I can fill up a cup for you. That'll be easier."

"No…" She dragged out the word. "I do it this way."

And there he stood, letting his PT's daughter drown herself in icy *foun-tan* water, braving brain freeze for fun.

"All done," she finally said, so he set her down and felt immediate relief. Now maybe he could get back to work.

"I have to pee."

He scrunched up his face, didn't even try to hide his reaction. Was this really happening? "Do you know how to do that by yourself?" Because there was no way he was getting involved in that.

"I'm almost five!" Up went the hand.

"Okay." Whatever that meant. He took her lifted hand, walked her to the unisex bathroom and nudged her inside. She gave him an exasperated glance, then pointed to the toilet seat cover container on the wall, too high for her to reach. He stepped inside, but only long enough to put the thin paper cover on the toilet, then turned to leave while again thinking how small she was and hoping she wouldn't fall in. Before he closed the door, she was already pulling down her leggings and underpants.

"Wait, wait, wait!" He couldn't help raising his voice, but seeing alarm on her face, he toned it down. "Let me leave first, okay?"

"Okeydoke." So easily appeased.

He stood outside the bathroom door for what seemed like forever, marveling at the innocence of children and how they needed to be protected. There went the stab to his heart again. He checked his watch, listening to make sure she hadn't fallen into that toilet bowl, but mostly wishing he was in his office doing what he was supposed to be doing. Unfortunately, his thoughts got stuck somewhere between loss and grief, pain and dangerously close to do-not-enter territory.

He pushed the feelings down, insisting he could do this. She was an innocent kid and he was the adult in the room. Soon he heard a flush. "I can't reach it!" she yelled.

He tried to open the door. How had she managed to lock it without him hearing? "Let me in so I can help."

"What?" she yelled over the running toilet water.

"Let me in." Instead of raising his voice, he lowered it, not wanting to draw attention to the predicament, or alert Keela that he'd already screwed up.

With the toilet flushing, she spent a few seconds opening the door, long enough to have Daniel wondering where he kept the emergency bathroom key. Once it was open, she beamed up at him as if she'd just completed the most amazing undertaking of her life.

Daniel stepped into the small bathroom and immediately turned on the water. "I'm going to teach you a trick," he said, putting the toilet lid down. "Stand on this." Anything to avoid holding her again.

She crawled up, then leaned forward to use the adjacent sink.

"See? Isn't that better?"

She tossed him a look that proved he was a true genius. But he still smarted from the last time he'd picked her up.

Anna clapped her hands beneath the stream of water. He jumped back to avoid getting wet, then guided her to the liquid soap and showed her how to lather up. "Make bubbles. That's how we doctors do it."

"You're smart!" Why did everything she say come out like an exclamation? Still, her compliment caught him off guard and he cracked a smile for the first time that afternoon. Okay, so she *was* kind of cute.

He glanced at his watch again. All of fifteen minutes had passed since he'd been handed the job of childcare provider, and Keela wouldn't be through until five. Now what should they do?

Keela stepped out of the therapy room, escorting her last patient back to the waiting room. She glanced in Daniel's office as she passed, but he and Anna weren't there. Worry flashed briefly. She followed the patient through the door and asked Abby where they were.

The receptionist didn't have a chance to respond before the front doors of the clinic flew open and in waltzed Daniel and Anna, half-eaten ice cream cones in their hands. He looked up, and rather than seem guilty about feeding a child ice cream right before dinnertime, his expression clearly read *Thank God you're done.*

Anna ran to her mother. "We had fun!"

"You did?" Surprised, she smiled, fixing her daughter's hair, tightening the lopsided bow and only then daring to look at Daniel again—who stood licking the remnants of his cone, ignoring both of them.

"Okay. So my job here is done," he said coolly, when he finally noticed her watching him. Then, business as usual, he walked to his office without another word.

She'd imposed her daughter on him, and what could she expect—that he'd love it? Thank the heavens it had ended well and she still had a job. But a flare of sadness made her think how Anna's own father hardly ever wanted to spend time with her. At least Daniel had taken her for ice cream, maybe not because he wanted to, but because he was a decent guy. That alone made him different from her ex.

"Say thank you, Anna." She guided her daughter to his office door, intent on showing her manners.

"Thank you!"

He looked surprised, maybe a little bothered by the interruption. Anything he'd done for her daughter had been purely out of duty, that was obvious. Maybe he wasn't so different from Ron.

"You're welcome. Okay, sport," he said nonchalantly, "remember to pump your feet out when you go forward and in when you swing back. Then you can swing really high." By the end of the sentence, he'd already gone back to focusing on his computer screen.

But that didn't seem to faze Anna. She gathered her backpack, put her crayons and coloring book inside, then zipped it.

Did he just say swing really high? How high? Keela

wondered, helping her daughter put her backpack over her shoulders. "Did you color Dad a picture?" she asked.

"No. We did lots of other stuff." Anna reached for her mother's hand, oblivious to Daniel's lack of attention, then let Keela lead her out the door. "He taught me to swing so high! He said I shouldn't 'spect him to do all the work."

"I didn't say it that mean," he interjected, without lifting his head.

So he *was* listening. Keela glanced over her shoulder at Daniel, in his own world, clacking away on computer keys, pretending to ignore them. *That guy taught you how to swing?* They continued down the hall.

"We looked at bugs and he let me hold a caterpillar and..." She babbled on with a lengthening list of everything they'd done. A surprisingly long list, too. *Daniel?*

"Is that so," Keela said, guiding her daughter toward the car.

Things didn't add up. Daniel couldn't have ignored Anna all afternoon and still won over her clear adoration. He'd taken her to the nearby park and bought her ice cream from the parlor three doors up. Shown her bugs and who knew what else. The child was practically dancing with joy. Of course, that could have something to do with the sugar high from the cone. Truth was, Anna never came home from the occasional visits with her father happy like this.

Keela tightened the belt on Anna's car seat, closed the back door and slipped behind the steering wheel, turning the key on the old but dependable sedan.

She had been under the impression that Daniel Delaney was a man driven by his profession. All his time and effort seemed to focus on the clinic, and she respected him for it. She'd heard from Abby about a bad breakup before he'd opened the business, as well as the terrible experience with the last PT, and understood why he might be standoffish with her, or any woman, for that matter. But even when he spoke brusquely to her, she never took it personally. She understood pain and what it did to people. She was part of his staff and wanted to see him succeed, not just for him, but for her job security. They were a team. She and Ron were anything but.

She pulled onto Main Street, passing the ice cream parlor where Daniel had bought Anna her treat, heading for her neighborhood several blocks inland from the beach.

Ron hadn't changed overnight. No, it had taken a couple years for his true personality to finally break through. He talked a good talk, but when it came to everyday living, the hard part of being a husband and providing for his family—for the woman he'd brought over from Ireland to be his lawfully wedded wife—he'd turned out to be selfish, demanding and miserable to be around. The fact that Anna hadn't been Andrew seemed suspiciously part of the problem. But mostly, once Keela learned there was no making him happy, she'd quit trying. She'd also quit holding back from pointing out his shortfalls. Things got ugly between them, and he spent more and more time away from home.

After he'd cheated on her, and they'd finally broken up, he'd agreed to pay for her to attend City College for a physical therapy assistant certificate. Payoff money? Guilt? Clearly, he'd wanted to get rid of her, especially since he'd found a new woman, this one a German exchange student. But Keela didn't care anymore; the old hurt had scarred over and in her heart she'd moved on. Never to be tricked by a sweet-talking man again.

She pulled into the carport beside her aging summer

cottage. After the divorce, she'd remembered her first trip to California and the quaint hotel on the beach in Sandpiper, and how much she'd loved it there. Since it was close to the college, she'd found this small place to rent and, though hurt to the core, did her best to get on with her life. Landing a job at the clinic had made a huge difference in her outlook.

Once released from her car seat, Anna flew out of the vehicle and ran like a whirlwind toward the porch. Keela stayed behind, gathering the backpack and her purse.

The day she'd first met Daniel Delaney, she'd tried her best to remain professional but knew her dire need for employment cracked through her job-applicant veneer. *Please hire me. Please. Please. Please?* His natural good looks had set her off-kilter, but she'd quickly focused beyond his shocking green eyes and his sturdy rugby build, the charming Irish smile she'd recognize anywhere. There was absolutely no reason for her to notice his stylishly cut, thick brown hair, but she had.

Thankfully, he'd hired her on the spot, and she'd promised herself to be the best employee she could possibly be for him. So if he seemed crusty or occasionally abrupt, he was allowed, and she let it roll off her back. That was nothing compared to the nonstop complaints she'd endured from her ex. Now she was part of Daniel's team. The businessman and doctor was helping her start her new life in the United States completely on her own.

She unlocked the front door while Anna jumped from one foot to the other, her sign for needing the bathroom.

Keela had saddled him with her daughter today and didn't expect him to appreciate it, but she'd been desperate, once again thanks to Ron. When would she learn she could never depend on that man? Daniel had obviously been unhappy about it, but he'd stepped up to the task and apparently had done far more than an adequate job, judging by Anna's cheery mood.

Anna lunged for the tiny pink-tiled bathroom. "Dr. Daniel taught me a trick today," she called over her shoulder.

"He did?" Keela followed her into the room.

After Anna finished her business, she grinned, shut the toilet lid with a bang and climbed onto it, then leaned over toward the nearby sink. "See?" she said as she turned on the water to wash her hands. "I can do this all by myself. I don't need that little kid's stool."

Keela had seen Daniel only as the man who'd hired her and saved her life until now, but today her predicament had pushed him out of the shadows and into the spotlight. And he'd sparkled. What was the saying? *Actions speak louder than words.* There had to be a lot more going on behind the gruff exterior of Daniel Delaney, because this afternoon, after first looking like he had a bad case of heartburn, the guy had turned out to be nothing short of a star.

After the rough ride with Ron, who'd changed bit by bit from wonderful to demanding, picky and never satisfied, then flat-out mean-spirited over their three-and-a-half-year marriage, she needed to believe there were still good men out there. Or, more realistically, regular guys with good hearts. Guys who could be trusted.

After Ron's painful betrayal and the divorce, and a year and a half of swearing off men, since she'd proved she had zero skills choosing the right type, something clicked. The thought scared her to no end, but she was a mature thirty-year-old mother now. She'd moved countries and survived. She'd learned to depend on herself and hadn't done such a bad job of it for her and Anna. Every day, she felt more confident, too.

She helped Anna dry her hands while her daughter babbled on.

Thanks to Ron, the mere thought of opening her eyes to what was around her, namely Daniel, still sent a jittery wave through her stomach.

Daniel finished assessing his last rescheduled patient, then went to his office, ready to pick up where he'd left off earlier, practicing his presentation for tomorrow, before he'd been interrupted by Anna. Even though the clinic was empty, he closed the door. The winding tangle in his chest since Anna walked in, reminding him of what he'd lost, pinched tighter. He sat, squeezed his eyes closed and, covering them with his hand, pressed his temples with thumb and fingertip. He stayed like that for a few moments, listening to his breathing, fighting off the pain, the grief, grasping at the calm that always eluded him at times like this. *Don't do it. Do. Not. Do it.*

But he didn't heed his own advice. Instead he opened the lower desk drawer, the one with the hanging files, riffling around way at the back until he found the manila envelope. He shook his head, knowing with every fiber of his being that he shouldn't, but he opened it anyway. Then carefully pulled out the ultrasound picture of Emma at twenty weeks. The day they'd found out she was a girl. A few days later, when a radiologist had given a proper reading of the procedure, something else even more significant was diagnosed.

The knot that had been twisting around his heart since Anna showed up tore loose as his eyes filled and Emma's perfect little profile went blurry. She'd never had the chance to drink from fountains, swing on swings, wear frilly tutus or even take a breath on the outside. And some days, like today, he was unsure if he'd ever get past the pain.

Chapter Two

Thursday midmorning, Keela was escorting her last patient before lunch to the reception room at the exact moment Daniel came bolting through the door, his smile broad enough to take flight. She glanced at his feet to make sure they weren't levitating.

He made eye contact and shot his fist in the air. "I did it!" he said through gritted teeth. "They hired me. Our clinic, I should say. Beginning next month, you'll have to give group physical therapy sessions, since we're going to be so busy with the City College jocks."

Keela clapped her hands. "That's fantastic!"

"I know! Let's celebrate. Abby, Keela, what do you say? Lunch at The Chinese Dragon, my treat."

An hour later, having overindulged on the delicious array of dishes Daniel had ordered, Keela finished her green tea and read her fortune cookie. She thought about her patient Joan Haverhill and the quick lesson she'd given on how to read them. "A smile is your passport into the hearts of others..." *In bed*, she added, then laughed inwardly, but it must have carried to her eyes.

"What?" Daniel said, nursing the last of his beer.

She crinkled her nose and shook her head. "Nothing." *Think fast and change the subject.* "Isn't it exciting that your pitch landed the deal?"

"I'm still in shock." He finished the celebratory longneck beer, looking a little absentminded. Obviously the guy wasn't used to drinking at lunch. He broke open his fortune cookie after paying the bill. "Well, would you look at this—'A dream you have will come true.' Who says fortune cookies are just a bunch of fluff?"

For a moment Keela gazed at Daniel, who didn't look away. She got the distinct impression he was seeing her differently, maybe for the first time? Neither blinked during the staring contest, until her heart thumped a quick run when an unwanted thought about his fortune slipped into her mind. *In bed.* Blink!

Abby opened her cookie, then grimaced.

Grateful for a reason to pull away from Daniel's deep green and enchanting eyes, Keela watched the fortysomething Abby—with her carefully quaffed and weaved blond hair and meticulously made-up eyes—read her fortune.

"'Land is always on the mind of a flying bird'? What does that even mean?"

They shared a group laugh, bellies full and spirits flying high, with a little something extra revving up on Keela's side of the table. Then they all got up as Daniel left an impressive tip for the waitstaff, and headed back to the clinic for the afternoon appointments.

* * *

An hour later, Daniel Delaney sat at his desk and pretended he hadn't noticed a single one of Keela O'Mara's attributes. Huge blue eyes? Nah, not his thing. Light brown, shoulder-length hair with gold spun through it? Nope. Never even registered. And that smile, where the sweetest and cheeriest disposition shone bright? Well, he did appreciate that—attributed it to her Irishness—but only because it made working with her as easy as the afternoon breeze off Sandpiper Beach. He laughed gently. Who said he couldn't be poetic? Besides, he'd need her dependability, since the quiet little clinic was about to get busy. Hallelujah.

He caught himself staring, elbow on his desk, leaning into his fist, practically drooling while daydreaming about Keela and the future of his clinic, then sat straight. Good thing he'd had a beer at lunch and could blame the shift in attitude toward Keela on that. The last thing he needed was to let his thoughts get out of control. The clinic was all that mattered.

Remember Kathryn, how she left you. If that didn't sober him up, nothing could. Relationships were a sticky process, and he wasn't the only one with a gut-wrenching history.

He totally understood that by their age, his being thirty-three and Keela's thirty, everyone, unless they were monks, seemed to have relationship track records, and those histories usually weren't good. Keela had taken back her maiden name, O'Mara, and her experience slanted toward disaster. As in love, marriage, betrayal and divorce. Yeah, he'd heard most of the story, because the walls were thin in his clinic and Keela was friendly with her clients, many of whom were women. If they dared to ask if she was married, she'd spout her well-rehearsed ten-second reply. *Met a man online, traveled all the way to America to meet 'im, fell in love, got married and had a kid all within a year. Now I'm happily divorced, thanks for asking.*

Or *"tanks for askin'"* as it sounded coming from those sweet lips. Nope, nope, nope, not supposed to notice those, either.

But that was the truth Daniel had to live with: a fellow American—*thanks a lot, buddy*—had soured the lovely Ms. O'Mara's view on men in general, and most especially *American* men, of which he was a card-carrying member. *Never again!* She'd often said that after getting off the phone chasing down yet another late child-support payment. The guy seemed like a total jerk and Daniel wondered what she'd ever seen in him.

He could totally relate to the *never again* part, thanks to Kathryn before she'd walked away…and he'd begged her to stay, to work things out. In fact, he and Keela could bond on their failed relationships. But he'd never dare discuss what had happened in his personal life with an employee. Only his family knew the whole story.

Ah, geez, all this thinking and overthinking had begun to make the room spin. Why had he had that beer with lunch? To celebrate, that was why, and he deserved it. He clicked on a patient file on his computer for distraction but had to wait while it loaded.

Was he looking? For another relationship? It had been almost two years since Emma had died and Kathryn had left. He dug his fingertips into his hair and gave a quick massage to ease the sudden tension sprouting at his temples and traveling upward, hoping it would help shake him out of this line of thinking. Instead of that happening, his personal stats popped up—thirty-three, still living at the family hotel, rooming with his brothers,

Mark and Conor, in a detached three-bedroom suite to save money—but costing his parents good cash, since they couldn't rent it out. Not exactly a prize, was he? He rationalized he'd be there only until his business was out of the infancy stage. Who knew how hard it would be to take a private practice and make it work? But he'd made great progress today. Soon his bookkeeping would go from red to black and he'd be able to move out of the hotel.

The patient file didn't have the specific information he was looking for, so he clicked on the medical history.

And while he scrolled through the abundant reports, he went back to thinking about women in general, to get his mind off Keela. He'd had many girlfriends, but he'd never been in a relationship that lasted more than two months. Until Kathryn. Even though being with her had struck the wrath of the universe on him. Kathryn had grabbed his attention the first time they'd met. The more he got to know her, the sexier she got, and they'd fallen into bed early on. She liked that he was a doctor, and he liked that she was not only a successful businesswoman, but personally independent. As it turned out, to a fault. An independent woman who wanted nothing to do with getting married, even after she'd accidentally gotten pregnant. Getting involved with a levelheaded woman might still be an aspiration one day, but only after he figured out the past. He'd loved Kathryn far more than she'd loved him. Turns out, after a man had his heart removed with surgical precision, it took a long time to grow one back.

He closed out the file, started searching through a pile of reports on his desk. A committed relationship would mean trying to live up to his parents', who seemed to have the ideal. His grandfather spoke about his Mary as if she'd been a saint. Daniel remembered his grandmother as being sweet and kind, and Grandda was definitely prone to exaggeration, but a saint? Still, the old man's face lit up with love anytime he mentioned her name.

Daniel had thought he'd found that kind of love with Kathryn, but he'd been astoundingly mistaken. He'd asked her to marry him within the first six months, long before she'd gotten pregnant, but she said she wasn't ready. He'd sensed her hesitation when it came to commitment, but like a fool, he thought they only needed more time together, as though two years wasn't long enough to make up her mind. After losing Emma, she'd withdrawn and pulled away. Weren't they supposed to cling together at a time like that? He'd done his best to support her, to reach out to her, even got her bereavement treatment. Her therapist said she needed time. Daniel gave it to her, but she didn't improve. She kept to herself and pushed him further and further away. Finally, she'd opened up and told him how she needed to be alone to heal, so even while drowning in his own pain and grief, needing her more than ever, he let her leave. Because that was what you did when you loved someone. He was hardly surviving, and in such pain over the loss of their baby he could barely work, yet he put her needs and wishes first. Alone, the pain so astounding he didn't think he could go on, he tried.

He'd always expected her to come back. He clung to the thought. But she never did. Then one day she'd sent for her things and delivered a cold and calculated goodbye letter. Last he'd heard, a year ago, she was in a relationship with someone new, and he wished her the best, he honestly did.

But Daniel was still stuck in limbo.

He no longer fooled himself about ever being able to find his parents' and grandparents' kind of love. He should've seen the signs early on, when Kathryn kept putting on the brakes whenever he pushed to get married. She wasn't into him in the same way, and he couldn't see it then. The memory sent a sharp pain through him. How had he not seen it? Because falling in love had blinded him.

After the shock and gut-wrenching trauma of losing what he'd held dearest, a family, he was nowhere near ready to look for a relationship again. He couldn't trust his instincts.

Man, he was frustrated—why couldn't he find that report? He shuffled a pile of papers around.

Keela popped into his thoughts again, her smile, her cheerful outlook.

And why was he still thinking about Keela? He should've noticed and heeded the not-so-subtle omen when his grandfather, after first hearing about his new employee, had said, "Did you know that the name Keela in Irish means 'beauty that only poetry can capture'?" Where did Gramps get that stuff?

Daniel glanced across his desk at another mound of papers, plus a patient appointment list that promised to keep him working until 8:00 p.m. These days the only commitment he could handle was his medical practice, a full-time job and relationship rolled into one, and it was all he could manage. There simply wasn't room for anything else. So here he was, working like a lunatic to get his business off the ground, with a PT assistant who'd started to lure his mind off the goal. He frowned and stared at his desk. Maybe that was why he was always gruffer with her than he intended. Self-preservation? *You bet.*

He sighed. Today had made everything different. He'd landed the City College account. He couldn't afford to take his eye off the prize. He shivered. What if he lost everything…again? He couldn't bear to think of the consequences. A kernel of apprehension over the future of his clinic quickly grew to full-out anxiety, which prompted him to call out. "Keela!"

She arrived in his office, sat, brows lifted, eyes sparkling like they had all through lunch. So alluring, so off-limits. Guilt filtered through him. *Nip the attraction in the bud, and file it under the heading of survival.* He swallowed and forged ahead, but not before noticing her delicate fingers lacing and unlacing in her lap. He'd made her nervous and he hadn't said a word. Already feeling like a heel, he so hated what he was about to do.

"So here's the deal," he said in a firm tone, skipping any niceties. "We're going to be challenged like never before with the City College athletes. I'll be spending time away from the clinic to attend their practices and games, and more responsibility will fall on your shoulders. So my question is, are you up for that?"

She sat on the edge of the chair in his office and nodded, her smile gone, a serious stare replacing the earlier glow. The power he wielded over her as her boss pinched behind his sternum, but he couldn't back down.

"I can't settle for excuses about back East weather holding up our supplies. It's unprofessional and can't happen again."

"I'll do my best to keep us stocked. If you give me the okay, I'll order far in advance or set up a standing order. It's just we've been counting pennies until now." Her fingers kept lacing and unlacing.

"Not anymore." This was his lifeline. The clinic had saved him after losing baby Emma, and when Kathryn no longer needed or wanted him. He shuddered when he considered what he might have done without the support of his family and this business venture to pull him through. This 4Cs deal gave him the chance to morph from struggling and heartbroken to successful businessman. His personal life might still be in shambles, but dammit, this clinic would shine because he was in control of this one thing. Work.

"From now on we have to work like a fine-tuned engine. Every minute will be put to good use. Last-minute childcare issues will be your issue, not mine. That can't happen again. Got it?" Because he might not survive spending another afternoon with her daughter and the heart-wrenching feelings it had brought up of Emma, innocent and helpless, and beyond his control to save.

How could he expect Keela to never have childcare issues or for the vendors to never screw up? She sat quietly, and he felt like an ogre reading her mind, but he continued full-on. "Can you deliver? Because your job depends on it." There, he'd said it—given her an ultimatum, his employee of the month, and he'd just entered the running for despicable boss of the year.

She looked stunned, anxious, chewing her lower lip as what he'd just said registered. "Yes. Of course." Insecurity had slipped into her voice.

"Good." She needed her job; what else could he expect her to say? *Bastard.*

He forced himself to look at her again. Seeing her squirm over the possibility of losing her job made him queasy, the mistrust he'd just planted in her usual open and honest gaze made him want to kick himself, but he ground his molars and kept quiet. She rose, serious and quiet.

He swallowed with difficulty. *Great going.* He'd just

successfully ripped the shine off their luncheon and put fear and dread into the best employee he'd ever hired.

Once she'd left, he followed her out of his office, on his way to the reception desk in hopes of finding a fresh pot of coffee. Hating how he felt, he swore to never have a beer at lunch again, no matter how much he had to celebrate. *What a mess.*

That evening, when Keela left for home, she didn't stop at his door to say good-night like she usually did. He'd been a complete ass, so what did he expect—Mother Theresa?

She didn't deserve to take the heat for her ex-husband hanging her up at the last minute, but Daniel had heaped it on her anyway. Wasn't the mark of a good boss compassion, and shouldn't a skilled businessman be able to find a balance between laying down the rules and reading a riot act? Sitting behind his desk, he dropped his head into his hands.

Spending an afternoon with Anna the other day had nearly been his undoing, seeing what he'd never have, grieving over a frilly tutu. Wishing life could be different. Then today, he and Keela had looked at each other in a special way during lunch. Beer or no beer, he'd felt that zing down to his toes. And for an instant he'd wondered if life *could* be different. The mere thought of opening up to a woman again had scared the egg rolls out of him, yet he'd considered it for that single moment. Just now he'd overcompensated for both instances by hiding behind the tough-boss act.

And it sure as hell didn't feel right.

Friday morning Daniel appeared at Keela's office door. She'd come in a few minutes early to make sure she was up to date with all her supply orders, and also to mentally prepare for her appointments lined up for the day. He looked…regretful maybe, or was that what she'd wanted to see because he'd been tough on her yesterday? "Hi," she said.

"Hi." He stepped inside. "Okay if I sit?"

"Of course." She stopped what she was doing to give him her full attention.

"I need to apologize for being a jerk. I was being unreasonable and I came down too hard on you yesterday evening."

"You were right, though. I wasn't assertive enough regarding the supplies. That company isn't the only one and I should have made some waves. And I should always have a backup plan where Ron is concerned. It was just that Mrs. Jenkins had that hair appointment." There she went, overexplaining out of insecurity. "I won't let that happen again. Promise." She said everything the way she'd practiced on her drive in that morning, fearing her job was at stake if she didn't.

"I thought I was supposed to be apologizing to you." He stared at her for a second while considering her carefully prepared explanation. "I won't let it happen again, either. Promise." Then he stood, turned and left.

After she'd married Ron and Anna had been born, Keela had tried hard to please him. She'd done it because she could tell his attitude toward her had changed. He'd *had* to marry her out of obligation, and though he'd never said it aloud, he'd always sent the subtle message: he was doing her a huge favor.

Just now, with Daniel, she'd fallen into an old and bad habit of bending over backward to please. But Ron had always managed to find fault somewhere, somehow, no matter how hard she'd tried. She was never good enough—like having a daughter instead of a son.

Once she'd made a mistake, he'd never let her off the hook. Eventually, she gave up even trying to please him, feeling such a failure, and he'd used that as an excuse to seek a relationship with someone else. Like it was her fault! Once a self-assured young woman, Keela had become unconfident, always doubting and second-guessing herself.

Now, under Daniel's scrutiny, she'd reverted to old habits. Maybe because all men were the same? But Daniel had apologized, then listened to her explanation and apologized again. In that regard, he was nothing like her ex.

Daniel finished his intake assessment of the quarterback of the 4Cs football team and arrived in his office to find the telephone light blinking.

"Your mom's on the phone!" Abby called from the reception desk, making him wonder how long she'd been on hold.

He'd been keeping busy all morning to avoid his thoughts about how he'd come off as a boss, how he'd intentionally intimidated Keela and how lousy he felt about it, and he knew any conversation with his mother would draw him back into the realm of the thinking and feeling. He considered asking Abby to tell her he was busy, but caught himself. Mom always knew when he was avoiding her.

"Hey, Mom, what's up?" He opted to sound rushed and on the run.

"Hope I'm not interrupting anything, but I've had a brainstorm and just wanted to run something by you."

"Okay."

"Dad and I have been discussing how to draw more visitors to the hotel this season, and I got the bright idea to add more amenities. You know, like massages and facials. My hairstylist has a part-time esthetician who would be willing to do some moonlighting, but I'm at a loss for where to find a massage therapist. You're kind of in that biz, right? Any thoughts?"

He pulled in his chin. He wasn't exactly in *that biz.* He didn't run a spa, but he did happen to know a former massage therapist turned PT tech. "Keela." For all the times she had to chase down her ex for child support, he figured she could use some extra money.

"Keela?"

In fact, the more he thought about it, the more he liked the idea. This would give him a reason to talk to her again, and to hopefully mend the damage he'd caused yesterday afternoon. He hated how things felt in the clinic today, all strained and quiet. Even though he'd apologized, he suspected that wasn't nearly enough.

"Yeah, Keela. Hey, I've got an idea. Why don't I bring her to Grandda's birthday party on Sunday and you can talk to her about it then. What do you say?"

"Sounds good to me. She has a daughter, right? Tell her to bring her, too."

"Sure thing." Daniel hung up feeling more positive than he had all day. Problem solved?

When Keela passed Daniel in the hallway, he gave a reassuring smile, the first she'd seen from him all day. Though it did seem forced, it was better than the grim face he'd been wearing. He didn't look like a man who wanted to fire her on the spot, which helped her breathe a bit easier. By her second-to-last appointment that day, there he was hanging out in her office doorway again. What was up?

He appeared uncomfortable, as if he might have to

tell her some bad news. More bad news? A sudden chill traveled up her spine. Insecurity made her wonder, what if he was going to fire her? She was still in the probationary period, and he had the right to call the shots on her future. Now the chill turned to a cold hard lump in her stomach. What would she do if he did?

"Are you available on Sunday?"

Wait, what? "Sunday?" Did he expect her to work weekends now, too? She would if it meant keeping her job.

He stepped inside her office but remained standing, a torn expression on his face.

"Yes, Sunday, it's my grandfather's birthday, and we're having a big party. I thought you and Anna might like to come. It's my way of trying to make up for being the boss from hell yesterday."

"Truly?" He'd just veered into completely different territory from Ron, who never even thought about apologizing, or doing something nice to make up for his actions.

"Thought maybe you two could use a day out with fresh air and good food."

The refreshing shift from "same old story" to "second verse, better than the first" buoyed her spirits.

"A party at The Drumcliffe?" She broke into a grin that came straight from her heart. Yeah, apparently she *was* that easy. "We'd love to come. Did I ever tell you I stayed at your hotel around six years ago, when Ron first brought me to visit?"

"You're kidding."

"I loved that place right from the start. That's why I came back here to live when we divorced. Paso Robles is okay, but it's too far inland. Plus I wanted to get away from him and his new lady." A burst of excitement had her talking more than she probably should, another old, hopefully not annoying, habit. But she'd just been asked out by her boss for a family gathering, and in her mind, that was a big deal. "Something about the cliffs and the ocean reminded me of Sligo Bay, back home. But it's much less rugged here. Anyway, I think your family owns a beautiful hotel."

"Wow. Small world. Well, I'm glad you like it. So you'll come, then?"

"Wouldn't miss it."

"Oh, another thing." He'd turned to leave, a pleased smile on his face, but paused. "No gift, okay? The old guy has everything he could possibly ever need. Your company will be more than enough." Daniel looked back, a new glint in those verdant green eyes. "I'll pick you up at one."

"You're picking us up?"

"I invited you, didn't I?"

Okay. Now what was she supposed to do with that? She fiddled with her hair, tucking one side behind her ear, a faint sense of happiness tingling in her chest. She wasn't getting fired, and he'd invited her to a family gathering. Was this an apology date?

Sunday turned out to be a gorgeous sunny spring day at Sandpiper Beach, and Keela hadn't been this excited about going somewhere in a long time. Anna was practically bouncing off the walls of the tiny and barely upgraded 1930s beach cottage.

"Yay, a birthday party."

"Remember, this is a grown-up party, so it won't be that much fun."

"Will there be games?"

"I don't think so, my love, but I'm sure there'll be cake."

"Yay! And ice cream?"

"What's a birthday without ice cream?" Keela hoped there'd be ice cream, otherwise she'd have to take Anna to the parlor near their clinic for a cone afterward.

Her daughter rushed to the cramped living room to peer out the window. "I like Dr. Daniel!"

He'd been surprisingly kind to Anna last Wednesday, even though at first he'd acted uninterested and maybe even a little put out about it. But thanks to her daughter's approval, and remembering that instant over lunch when something special seemed to click between them, Keela had taken a second look at her boss. The other day, he'd reminded her of Ron, but then he'd apologized and veered into new territory with the invitation. Maybe she liked Dr. Daniel, too?

Butterflies fought for territory in her stomach as she smoothed her hands over her hair and checked her makeup in the mirror of the tiny pink-tiled bathroom. Too much? Not enough? Oh, what did it matter? Daniel Delaney hardly knew she existed. Beyond being a good employee, that was. The invitation was his way to apologize for taking his usual moderately gruff self and upgrading to outright brusque. Sure, she'd noticed, and it didn't make a lot of sense, especially after their fun lunch together. But once she'd realized he hadn't planned to fire her, she was fine with whatever he needed to do. This wasn't a date. The man always seemed to go out of his way to avoid looking at her, unless they had specific patient care to discuss. Yet Thursday over Chinese food he'd watched her with clear interest, nearly nonstop.

His deep brown hair was straight and thick, and she

liked how he wore it swept off his forehead and neatly trimmed around his ears and neck. But what she liked the most was his Irish grin, wide and friendly, reminding her of being back home. She hadn't noticed it before lunch on Thursday, since he rarely smiled like that at work.

He was medium height, maybe five-ten or -eleven, but far taller than her five foot three. She always had to look up to see his eyes. She took a quick inhalation. Oh, those eyes, moss-green and downright swoon-worthy… But wait, she didn't do that anymore—think about guys. Or swoon. After the heartbreak she'd been through with Ron, and the divorce, no man was worth it. Besides, Daniel was her boss. Only a fool would risk her job by getting involved with the boss.

Anna had to come first these days. Nothing else mattered.

Keela's phone rang, and when she saw it was her ex-husband, her earlier hopeful mood slumped. What would he be calling about? Ever since his girlfriend, Ingrid—the woman who'd brought about their divorce—had given birth to their *son*, it seemed Ron had lost interest in Anna.

Stiff upper lip. "Hey, Ron, what's up?"

"Thought we'd pick Anna up and take her to lunch with us."

"Oh, shoot, any other day would've been great, but we've got a birthday party to go to." Why today? He frequently skipped his visitation days, like last Wednesday, and this wasn't the usual weekend they'd agreed to, even though he'd never come to get her since the baby was born. Now, out of the blue—

"There'll be other birthday parties," he said. "It's time she met her little brother."

She could have done that on Wednesday, eejit. Keela had to think fast, since she knew how he always insisted on getting his way. "Oh, yes, I think she'd love to meet her little brother, Diesel." The baby had to be nine or ten months by now. "But she's been looking forward to this party so much. She's dressed and ready to go. How about next Saturday or Sunday? She could sleep over, even—that is if you wanted her to." Keela also knew not to push Anna on Ron, or he'd pull back even more. The fact that he'd seemed to have nearly forgotten their daughter since he'd had his son made Keela's heart squeeze. "Would that be all right?"

Silence. "Ron, are you there?"

"We'll see about next weekend. Okay, gotta go."

Just like old times, she'd messed up and he'd gotten ticked off. He hung up before Keela could say goodbye, probably avoiding giving her a chance to mention he was late *again* with his child support payments—was that why he'd skipped out on Wednesday? But that didn't matter nearly as much as his not even bothering to ask to speak to Anna. That was his routine. If he didn't get his way, someone had to pay, and today it was her sweet and completely innocent daughter.

Keela had gotten bloody good at taking his crap, but Anna *never* deserved it. *To hell with that stiff upper lip.* Her chin quivered on her daughter's behalf, and her eyes blinked several times. She took a quick inhale, hoping to recover. Anna couldn't see her like this; it would upset her. Thankfully, she'd had the conversation in the bathroom, and her eager daughter was still keeping watch at the front window. What she didn't know couldn't hurt her.

"Mom! Dr. Daniel's at the door!"

A surprising burst of excitement lit up Keela's chest—

Daniel was here—helping her forget about the call. She wiped at her eyes and did a quick once-around in front of the full-length mirror on the bathroom door, ensuring her tan pants didn't make her backside look too big, and that her tank top with a matching camellia-pink sweater didn't show too much on the topside. Were her earrings okay? Would it be too much if she slipped on a bracelet?

What was going on with her? It wasn't like it was a date. It was the continuation of an apology, though this would be the first time she'd ever been with Daniel around his family. Would he be different? He was always so serious at work.

"Mommy, he's knocking!"

Keela sucked in a breath. *Come to your senses.* She rushed to the door and, trying not to seem too eager, opened it and peeked around the corner. "Hiya."

"Hey. You ready?"

Not for what she saw standing before her. Sure, she'd seen him in the medical clinic's uniform of khaki cargo pants and white polo shirt five days a week, and he'd worn a suit the other day for his pitch session at the college. But today he wore straight-legged jeans with a pale green, collared, long-sleeved shirt and a skinny dark green tie, looking very trendy. The button-down shirt was narrow cut and hugged his torso, giving her the impression he possessed something along the line of washboard abs. She forced her gaze upward to his still-smiling face, seeing something different in his eyes, too. Apparently, while she'd been checking him out, he'd done the same, and now her palms tingled.

"I'd invite you in, but there's not much to see." The "cottage" was more like a bungalow, with tiny rooms, kitchen and bath, but it was their home.

"Not a problem. You're looking great, by the way,"

he said, seeming on the verge of saying more. But Anna launched herself from behind.

"Hi. Remember me?"

"How could I forget?"

"How old is your granddad?"

"He'll be eighty-five today."

"Wow, is he alive?"

Daniel laughed. "Very much so. Are you ready to go meet him?"

"Yay!"

Even though Daniel played along with Anna and their quick conversation seemed to come easily, Keela sensed something behind his smile. Tension of some sort? Pain? It made her wonder what his story was about children.

They arrived at The Drumcliffe Hotel in a few short minutes, Anna chattering the entire ride, relieving any guilt Keela harbored about not letting her see her father today. She felt a little sad, though, realizing how much her daughter enjoyed people. And since the divorce, what with Keela now working full-time and going to school before that, Anna didn't get to go out that much.

Mrs. Jenkins, an older neighbor lady, had offered to do childcare for practically a song on weekdays when they'd first moved in, which was a huge help, but Anna didn't have anyone to play with. If Keela could afford it, she would've liked to put her in private preschool, but that was out of the question. She wouldn't dare ask Ron for more money. At least in the fall she'd start kindergarten and would be around kids her age then. Life was far from perfect, but good enough, and today promised to be special. What more could Keela ask?

Daniel pulled into a reserved parking space near one of the secluded suites. The two-story hotel sat on prime beachfront property and was the main tourist site in tiny Sandpiper Beach. Though she hadn't visited since moving back to town, Keela remembered it well. It seemed a mystery why such a lovely place had trouble renting rooms. The problem was, she had heard, visitors chose to either continue up the road to Carmel or stop first in Pismo Beach, rather than venture into this sleepy little town. But they didn't know what they were missing. Sure, the hotel seemed a bit dated, in need of some sprucing up, yet the potential was obvious. To Keela, anyway.

A narrow walkway lined with manicured shrubs separated the hotel from the beach, and nearly all the second-story guest rooms had a magnificent sea view. *So much potential.* To the right of the hotel was a large grassy area with a putting green, surrounded by palm trees and bushes, and beyond that the dunes. In honor of the birthday and the many guests, they'd set up several round tables with built-in umbrellas. Groups of people milled about, wearing bright springtime colors that complimented the grass, light blue sky and teal-colored ocean backdrop. Keela would never get tired of the sound of the sea, or that special salted scent.

She inhaled, remembering why she loved this town so much. Finding and moving to Sandpiper Beach had been the one good thing about getting her divorce, leaving Ron inland and moving to the coast.

"There he is, Oh Danny Boy. How's the form? Are y'well?" someone called out.

For an instant, at the sound of the familiar brogue, Keela thought she was back in Ennis. She nearly laughed aloud when she glanced up to see an old fellow speed-walking across the lawn in bright green knickers with high socks, a yellow-and-green argyle-patterned sweater vest and a newsboy cap jauntily sitting atop his thinning crop of white hair. Why did men enjoy dressing in strange costumes for a game of golf? Using his putter as a cane as he approached, Daniel's grandfather was certainly a vision from the past.

"Get ready," Daniel said out of the corner of his mouth to Keela. "Grandda! Happy birthday to ya."

Now even Daniel had a touch of the Irish to him. Keela's smile doubled as a home-sweet-home feeling circled around her like a hug.

"Is this the lovely lass from Éire?"

"Yes," Daniel said. "This is Keela." He glanced at her with a sweet and proud grin that she'd never seen before, and momentarily, she felt off balance.

"'Tis a pleasure, Keela!" The elderly man grabbed her into a bear hug, and laughing, she hugged him back. He smelled like Guinness and her own grandfather's spicy men's cologne, and a pang of nostalgia threatened to make her eyes tear up, though she fought it.

"So nice to meet you, too, Mr. Delaney." She saw the familiar twinkle she'd noticed in Daniel's eyes earlier, and the same brackets around his grinning mouth. There was no doubt they were family.

"Call me Padraig, please." He stood there leaning on his golf club, taking her in and seeming to appreciate what he saw. Then his gaze shifted to her side. "And who might this little elf be?"

"My daughter, Anna."

"Hello, lassie." He bent over, took Anna's hand and shook it. She giggled. "What age are ya?"

"Five." Up went the splayed-fingered hand.

"Almost," Keela added.

"Almost five. Are we gonna have cake and ice cream?"

He blurted a laugh. “Oh, you bet. We Delaneys know how to throw a birthday party, now, don’t we? Why don’t you let me show you the cake?” With her hand firmly in his, they set off toward a big table on the hotel patio that held a huge cake and a punch bowl. A large, built-in barbecue was going full blast behind the table, the mouthwatering aromas of grilled tri-tip and chicken competing for her attention.

“He’s full of life, isn’t he?” Keela couldn’t help her grin.

“Oh, he’s full of it, all right,” Daniel said, following his grandfather toward the table and a group of people gathered there. The redheaded woman, she assumed, was his mother.

Keela’s smile continued to stretch wide, threatening cheek cramps, as her boss dutifully introduced her first to his father, Sean. She’d gathered from the way he spoke about his dad at work that he respected him and considered him to be his business mentor. The man stood a great deal taller than his son and had a prominent chiseled nose. Where Daniel had an oblong chin, Sean’s was squared. Plus Daniel’s eyes were green, his father’s deep blue, serious and calm like the sea. Her smile leveled out as she summed him up to be a man content around his family. And she also decided Daniel had taken after his mother in the height department.

“This is my mother, Maureen.” He gestured toward the lady with ginger-colored bobbed hair and emerald-green eyes—so that was where Daniel got them.

Maureen took Keela into a light, welcoming hug, then quickly released her. “So glad you could come.”

“I’m happy to be here.”

“I hope my son has been treating you right.”

“Oh, he’s a great boss.”

Maureen tossed her son a proud glance tinged with motherly concern, but he'd already started a conversation with his dad, no doubt retelling how he'd sealed the deal with the 4Cs.

"I've got a question for you," Maureen said. "Does your physical therapy certificate include massage therapy, by any chance?"

"In a roundabout way, yes. My job description includes mostly PT treatments, which includes massage, but it just so happens that back home I was a certified massage therapist. That's what I did before I returned to school after Anna was born."

"Great. We should talk over lunch."

That piqued Keela's interest but also set off a burst of disappointment—was that why Daniel had invited her today? Just when she was about to ask more, Padraig scooted Anna forward. "And this is the lovely Miss Anna, Keela's daughter."

Maureen dropped to a knee to greet Anna eye to eye, the gesture planting warmth in the center of Keela's chest, pushing aside the prior disappointment. No wonder Daniel was such a good guy—he'd come from a wonderful family.

She felt warm fingers lightly circle her upper arm. Daniel. His touch made her skin tingle. "Let me introduce you to my brothers."

Two strapping men stood nearby, drinking sodas and chatting, and Daniel led her toward them while Anna happily talked with Maureen and Padraig Delaney as if she'd known them all her short life.

"Mark, this is the best physical therapy assistant in Sandpiper Beach, Keela O'Mara."

"Is my brother treating you right?" The intense blue-eyed man attempted a smile as he shook her hand, but

Keela got the impression that particular expression didn't come easy for him. He was a couple of inches taller than Daniel and wore his dark hair similarly, straight back from his forehead, though longer and with waves, but his two-day growth of beard made for a completely different look. Mysterious and sexy. She'd never thought of Daniel as sexy, but seeing him today had definitely put him in a new light. Now, having met their father, she understood where the Delaney appeal came from.

"I love my job. Thanks. And nice to meet you."

"Same here." He was obviously a man of few words, the strong silent type, she guessed, but regardless, she liked him right off.

"And this guy's my baby brother, Conor." Daniel mock-punched the tallest of the three brothers in the stomach, and Conor pretended to feel pain.

A thought popped into her head: What was it like to be the oldest yet the shortest? Maybe that was why Daniel worked so hard to prove himself all the time.

"Hello. I hear you're a deputy sheriff," she said, completely able to see him in uniform, what with his height, straight shoulders and light brown, military-length hair. Handsome with a strong jaw and chin like his father's, plus a pair of shockingly blue-green eyes, Conor could star in movies.

"I am. Nice to meet you."

"I thought you had to work today," Daniel said.

"I start at three."

For having Irish in their blood, neither Mark nor Conor seemed to have inherited the gift for gab. And they kept passing her sideways glances, the protective kind families sometimes give. More fingers wrapped around her arm. These were icy and knobby and belonged to the birthday boy himself, and feeling herself the center of attention, Keela grinned.

Daniel watched his family as they met and assessed his assistant. It wasn't hard to tell they all liked what they saw. Who wouldn't? But they also surreptitiously watched him, reading more into his bringing a woman around than his need to apologize. Especially a woman with a child. Were they worried? He'd once given them a hell of a lot to worry about. Kathryn had taken his heart and slammed it on the mat, nearly finishing him, and he still winced, remembering. Like he didn't mean squat to her, when he'd given her his whole heart. He'd limped around in a trance for months when he'd first moved home, the woman and baby he'd dreamed about and intended to spend the rest of his life with having vanished. His family knew he was still in deep healing mode, so he'd cut them some slack if they worried about him today.

He'd proposed to Kathryn the day she'd told him she was pregnant, but she'd sworn she would never get married because she "had" to. In his love-blind state, he'd rationalized they could get married after their baby was born. Ceremony or no ceremony, they would soon be a family. Maybe then she'd see how deeply he loved her and love him back. He wanted to give her a ring, but she'd begged him to hold off, reasoning they'd need the money for medical expenses during the pregnancy. He'd gone along with all her reasons, refusing to see the truth, even while sensing and fearing she wasn't the least bit invested in him. What a blind fool he'd been.

He'd gone inward, Daniel realized, and everyone seemed to notice.

"Would you like to see our pub, Keela?" Grandda

had grabbed her arm, looking eager to show her around, to get her away from the ball of gloom Daniel had just become.

"I'd love to."

Grandda laughed with delight and led Keela away. How effortlessly she'd fit in with his family. Daniel's chest flooded with adrenaline, an anxious thought quickly following. What the hell did he think he was doing, bringing a woman back into his life? A woman with a child.

Little fingers tugged at his. He looked down, to find Anna smiling up at him. The smile may as well have been a dagger. But she didn't deserve his reaction. He forced himself to look at her. She had wildly wavy brown hair along with those dark eyes she must have inherited from her father, yet the smile clearly belonged to her mother, and the combination made her one cute kid. The vision hit like a wrecking ball to what was left of his heart. Emma, sweet, sweet Emma, had never stood a chance, yet from the start he'd let himself imagine being her father years down the line, her wearing little girlie dresses just like Anna's ruffled brown-and-peach-colored combo today.

It had been nearly unbearable to spend time with Anna the other day, so he'd kept her busy and himself distracted. Now the sight of her, the feel of her tiny, warm hand, tightened his chest to the point of nearly being unable to suck in a breath. He searched around for an exit strategy. But with Keela heading off with his grandfather, this one needed supervision.

He didn't want the job by any means, even thought about pawning her off on Conor, but he'd invited her, and a kid couldn't understand a grown man's grief. Plus she'd apparently been ignored by her own father enough already. The last thing Daniel wanted to do was play a part in a lifetime of insecurity. She was an innocent and clueless child, just like Emma had been. So he needed to man up and stuff all his loss deep down, where it belonged, for an afternoon at a birthday party. He'd deal with the fallout later.

His eyes frantically darted around the hotel yard, soon finding what he looked for.

"Want to meet my dog?" What the hell, he'd give it a try. Maybe Daisy would distract Anna enough to keep her from holding his hand again.

"Our dog," his brothers chimed simultaneously.

"*Our* dog, Daisy." He couldn't exactly contradict them, since he'd gotten the puppy for therapy, a last attempt to rejoin the human race. That was before he realized how much time and energy his medical clinic would take. It didn't seem fair to the poor, sweet Labrador retriever puppy to be left alone for such long periods of time. So he'd asked Mark, who seemed to need a companion while working through his PTSD last year, to watch her during the days. And Conor, who took pride in staying in shape, ran their girl on the beach every single morning. When Mark and Conor weren't about, his mother let Daisy follow her around the hotel as a petting dog, a novelty that the guests seemed to love. Especially when she wore a glittery kerchief. Even Grandda had been known to let the dog accompany him on his strolls down Main Street. So, in the case of Daniel's pet, it seemed to take a village to raise her.

"A dog? Yes!" It didn't take much to excite Anna.

"Well, let's go, then."

A couple hours later, birthday toasts had been made, lunch had been eaten and cake had been served. And

Daniel had survived more time with Anna. Though barely. Keela had been whisked away yet again, this time by his mother. He wondered what Keela might think of his mom's forthcoming offer. Conor had left for work, but thankfully, Padraig Delaney was currently teaching Anna how to use a Hula-Hoop. Daniel was grateful for the break. Eighty-five to almost five, no big deal, they got along like best friends.

Sitting on a bench near the patio on the grass, Daniel tried to focus on the positive in his life—he'd landed the deal with the college. The weather was holding, and after the huge lunch, he needed a walk by the beach. So he took off.

"Where're you going?" Keela called out from nowhere.

"Thought I'd walk to the dunes. Want to come?"

"Love to. Let me get Anna."

All his positivity plummeted to the grass as she loped toward her daughter, surprising her, grabbing her under the arms and swinging her around in a circle, to Anna's delight.

They seemed so happy, and Daniel couldn't deny they had something special going on. He suspected the divorce had been rough on both of them, and their bond had tightened as a result. He, on the other hand, had been left with a longing so deep for what they had, it had eaten him from the inside out, leaving an empty shell. What losing Emma hadn't ripped away from him, Kathryn's leaving without a glance back had demolished.

Daisy came galloping up. Adopting her had been his futile attempt to begin to feel again. He ruffled her ears, welcoming the contagious calm she always brought. Since Anna was coming, he decided to bring the dog along for the walk, too.

Once Keela and Anna caught up, he pointed in the direction he'd decided to take across the dunes toward the cliffs and tide pools. Give a man a task and he would carry it out. This he could do—lead the excursion. Anna ran ahead with Daisy, and he and Keela found themselves alone for the first time all afternoon.

"Your grandfather told me a very interesting story," she said as they strolled over the sand.

"About the time I was five and tried to eat a baby frog?"

"No! You did?" She elbowed his arm when she realized he was joking. "Anyway, he's a funny man. Very sweet." After a few more steps down the dunes, the waves crashing in the distance, she continued. "He said you and your brothers went deep-sea fishing one morning, and he insists you saved a selkie." She glanced at him, her lashes batting her cheeks, teasing, testing, challenging him to give her an answer.

"I don't even know what a selkie is. I should've warned you about him." He quickened their pace.

"It's Irish folklore." She worked to keep up. "A selkie lives as a seal in the sea but can become a woman or man on land. He said you saved a seal from a pod of orcas."

"And what if we did?" It was his turn to tease and test her, to see how much Grandda had told her.

"The selkie owes you a favor. Padraig insists you're all going to find wives soon because of it."

Daniel clapped a palm to his forehead. Couldn't he have kept that part to himself? "Sometimes he is so embarrassing. I told you he's a wee bit touched, didn't I?" Daniel's Irish accent was lousy, though he hadn't really tried.

"No, you didn't, but I think it's sweet of him to want

his grandsons married. You did save a seal, after all. I guess he's allowed his own interpretation of the event. How did you save it, anyway?"

Daniel took a deep breath, trying to remember the exact events of that day close to a year ago. "The poor seal had been singled out by the orcas. They wear down their prey by playing with it, taunting it. It's really hard to watch. Anyway, we started our boat and moved closer to the pod. Probably a really stupid thing to do, in retrospect, but the noise distracted the orcas and that gave the seal a chance to get away. Then we moved our boat between the orcas and the seal, helping her—I mean *it*—escape. Looking back, I realize that could have been disastrous. *Don't try this at home, kids.* Like I said, we were stupid trying such a stunt, but we did it nevertheless."

"Still, it's an amazing story."

"Not really. We just wanted to take Mark deep-sea fishing because he was down in the dumps after he got out of the army." *I was hardly holding on at the time, too. Come to think of it, so was Conor.* "We didn't have any plans to be heroes or anything. I guess our biggest mistake was telling our family about it at the pub that night, over Sunday dinner."

"Well, you certainly made an impression on your grandfather."

"Fanciful thinking, as my father calls it. But we all tolerate it because, well, it's Grandda."

"Padraig insists you'll all find someone, because freeing a mermaid brings good luck in love."

Ha! That's a good one. "The seal was a mermaid?"

"Have to admit I've never heard that part of the folklore meself." It was her turn to laugh lightly, catching him off guard, as always, with the lilting sound. "Usually the selkie stories I've heard are very dark and sad."

Well, that's just great. And suitable for the three damaged Delaney brothers. We've all been unlucky one way or another. We're all fighting our way back from something.

And it was his turn to change the subject. "How'd things go with my mom?"

"Terrific." He could see true and immediate enthusiasm in her eyes. She wasn't just being polite. "Your mother wants me to work for her on the weekends, giving massages to guests. She said she'd buy the massage table for me, and the appointments would be in the guest rooms at first, until she can find a spot for a mini spa." Where he and his brothers were currently living would be the perfect place, but, well, they were all living there. "She said the tips alone would be worth it. She even offered to watch Anna while I was at the hotel. I'm pretty sure I can work this out. That is, if you're okay with it?"

"If you think taking on the extra work is worthwhile, I'm happy to let you figure out your own schedule. But won't spa massages take more time away from her?" He pointed to Anna up ahead, giggling and running on the uneven dunes with Daisy as if they were best friends.

"I've had to scramble to make ends meet sometimes, and I hate depending on undependable Ron, so if I work more efficiently, it shouldn't be too much more time and will be well worth the effort. Besides, she'll be right there at the hotel when I'm there."

"You can always try it out and see how it goes. No harm, no foul. I want what's best for you, so that being said, maybe it would be easier all around if I just gave you a raise." He wasn't sure he could offer much right away, but if it helped make her life less complicated…

"Thanks, but I agreed to that salary for one year when you hired me, right? Besides, I'm looking forward to branching out. I used to really enjoy being a massage therapist."

Jumping right into stereotypical male fantasies, Daniel wondered what it might be like having her hands and fingers touching him. He tried to stop the vision, but he was weak—what could he say, he was a guy—especially with her looking so beautiful today.

It hit him. This was the first time since Kathryn that he'd been remotely interested in a woman. Which lit a whole new fire of fear under him. Since he'd already faced several demons today, he may as well be honest and admit he was far beyond the interest stage, and halfway to knee deep in infatuation with Keela O'Mara. *Just great.* And the last thing in the world he needed right now.

Had he turned into a glutton for pain? Even entertaining the possibility of letting any type of relationship, from platonic on up, occur seemed the path to hell on earth. Yet here he was, thinking how beautiful she looked, how the ocean mimicked her eyes. Plus the fact she hadn't run off screaming with her hair on fire when his grandfather insisted on telling her a selkie had ensured his grandboys would all be married soon.

"Did I ever tell you you're the best boss I've ever had?"

Boss. *Yes!* Employee. Boss-employee would be his angle, or in this case, his saving grace. "Ha! You mustn't have had too many jobs." He hoped his face didn't betray the thoughts he'd just conjured up.

She offered a sweet smile that made his chest thump. Damn, this had to stop. He glanced ahead to dilute the potency of the moment. *Boss. Employee.* That "what if" feeling couldn't go *anywhere*. He was just beginning to get back on his feet, to feel half-human again. He'd been down heartbreak lane, suffered excruciating pain, been emotionally decimated and was still dealing with the fallout.

"We better catch up with them." Without thinking, he reached for her hand and started a slow jog. Then, with her palm flat against his and feeling far too intimate, he realized what a mistake that was. Especially after what he'd just been imagining about her hands. He couldn't exactly drop it now, though; he'd have to at least wait until they'd caught up with Daisy and Anna. *Quit overthinking everything. Just keep jogging, idiot.*

Here's a thought: enjoy yourself.

Anna and Daisy romped over the dunes, the child never quite able to catch up. She laughed and called after the pup, who kept running, so she ran harder and faster. Daniel worried they were getting too far ahead, so he picked up his step, Keela keeping pace.

Daisy leaped over something and landed on the other side, and Anna didn't even try to stop.

In the next instant, she disappeared.

Chapter Three

Daniel dropped Keela's hand and sprinted toward the spot on the dunes where the child had vanished. Keela shouted Anna's name as she ran behind him.

"Anna!" Daniel also called out. He heard cries and screams in answer. Memories of Emma, tiny and helpless, flooded his thoughts. With his pulse pounding in his ears, his breathing hard, he arrived at the edge of the slope. Anna lay at the bottom, at least eight feet below, on rocks and in tidewater. He climbed down the side and, slipping into doctor mode, immediately realized she'd broken her left leg when she'd hit bottom. A compound fracture. The jagged bones sliced through her skin, and she had a deep gash higher up, which bled rapidly.

"I'm here." Though breathless, he tried to reassure the panicked child. "Let me take a look."

Anna, her eyes squeezed tight with tears pouring

out, held still as though afraid to move, though unable to stop trembling. Daniel's stomach twisted into knots as he fought a flood of anxiety. He focused on her injury, his first hope that the bone hadn't nicked an artery.

"Anna!" Keela had made it to the edge of the drop-off.

"Mommy!" she wailed. A good sign.

"Do you have your cell phone?" Daniel shouted as he undid his tie and ripped off his shirt to press on the gushing blood above the open break. He'd left his in the car.

"No. I left everything back at the picnic."

"Go get help. I'll take care of this."

"What's wrong?"

"She's broken her leg."

Keela gasped. He left out the profuse-bleeding part so as not to freak her out even more.

"Mommy!" the child screamed. Lungs still strong, no sign of shock or loss of consciousness setting in. She was able to lift her head and move her hands. Good. Her leg, and not her spine, had taken the brunt of the fall.

"You're going to be okay, Anna, sweetheart." Keela's voice quavered. "Daniel will take care of you, and I'll be back as soon as I get help. I love you." Without another word she sprinted back toward the hotel, Daisy staying behind on the other side of the gully, pacing back and forth.

Daniel put pressure on the gushing wound, all the while attempting to say soothing words to the hurting and frightened child. "You're going to be all right. I'm here. Mommy's going for help. She'll be right back."

Heartbreaking memories flashed through his mind of consoling Kathryn when the unthinkable had happened with Emma. First the ultrasound, the congenital heart defect diagnosis. Then the day Kathryn thought labor pains were Braxton Hicks, not the real thing, until she'd given birth to their barely twenty-two-week-old baby on the bathroom floor. Far too early for Emma to survive. But Daniel had delivered their daughter and held the tiny, limp body close to his chest, bargaining his own life for hers, his grief echoing off the bathroom tile. *If there is any way to save her...please.*

Anna sobbed and reached for him. He thought fast and applied his tie above the area of bleeding for a makeshift tourniquet, then tightened it. He wrapped his shirt around the compound fracture to protect it from more sand and seawater getting inside the open wound, never letting up on the area that bled. Then, with his other arm, he hugged her close, lifting her. "You're going to be okay."

"Don't leave," she whimpered.

The plea melted his heart. "Not a chance. I'm right here." He held her tight, looking for a way out. The only possibility led toward the ocean, since there was no way he could climb the side of the steep slope while holding a child. Heading toward the beach was a huge challenge, but doable, since it was low tide. But only if he didn't lose his footing on the slippery rocks and possibly do more damage to her leg. But most important, only if he kept his wits about him. He wouldn't let Anna down. He couldn't.

If the bone had nicked an artery, time was precious; he had to move and move fast. Nothing would stop him from saving her. Nothing. With a deep inhalation, he willed himself the strength to safely carry her out of there, and in record time. Her eyes closed. "Stay with me, honey. Are you okay?"

She nodded instead of answering, whimpering all

the while. Alarmed by her suffering, he sped up as he followed the low tide toward the beach, holding on to Anna for dear life. He remembered Emma's tiny body, how fragile and precious she'd been. How he couldn't save her because she'd been born too early and with a fatal heart defect. Tears streamed down his cheeks as he made his way, clumsily slipping on rocks here and there, but never letting go of Anna no matter how awkward.

She felt far more substantial than his baby had. Nothing would prevent him from getting her to the lifeguard station and then to the hospital ER. He glanced down at her leg—the bleeding seemed to have slowed a bit. Though she was broken, she would mend, as long as the blood loss was controlled and he delivered her to where she needed to be. He could do that. He *would* do it.

But tiny Emma had never had a chance.

Keela sat with Daniel in the hospital waiting room three hours later, while Anna was in surgery. With every last nerve soundly jangled, she bit on her thumbnail, hoping for a word soon from the on-call orthopedic surgeon. As a doctor, Daniel had obviously pulled some strings to speed things along. She didn't know what she would have done without his help.

Her memories were mostly a blur. He'd carried Anna halfway back to the hotel by the time lifeguard help had arrived, and soon after, the ambulance. He'd stayed by her daughter's side like her own personal angel throughout the ambulance ride and ER visit, helping Keela keep it together whenever she'd fallen apart. Once here, he'd been her voice for the doctors and nurses when she'd been too emotional to make any sense, and also her mother hen, tending to her every need. Water. Coffee. Suggesting that bathroom break. Now, sticking around when he didn't have to, he'd quickly become her superhero.

"I just heard about the accident." Conor Delaney in full deputy sheriff uniform rushed into the surgical waiting room, concern blazing in his eyes.

"They're doing an ORIF," Daniel said.

"Layman's terms, please."

"Open reduction internal fixation. They reduce the fracture, then hold the bones in place with screws and plates so they can heal and grow back together."

Conor grimaced. "That doesn't sound fun."

Keela's stomach knotted tighter at the thought of what her baby was going through.

"She'll have a long recovery, and infection will be a major concern."

Oh, God, they were nowhere near out of the woods.

"Tough luck. Wow. I'm so sorry." He glanced at Keela with an empathetic expression. Pulling herself together yet again, she mustered a wan smile. Then he nodded at his brother. "What happened to your shirt? You on staff here now?"

Daniel glanced down as if just realizing he'd been without a shirt when they'd first arrived and he'd had an ER nurse grab a scrub top for him. The fact that he'd been shirtless for the entire ambulance ride hadn't gone unnoticed by Keela, either, and she'd been right about the washboard abs. *Strange what a person notices in crisis mode.* Under the circumstances, it felt so wrong to be aware.

Seeing Conor Delaney in uniform also proved her earlier suspicion, and Keela did her best not to stare at the man. So these Delaney brothers were *all* hunks. She winced inwardly at the contemptable thought, considering her daughter was having emergency surgery.

Being around two men, it hit her that she hadn't called Ron. For distraction while the brothers talked, she dialed her ex-husband's number. Doing her best to pull it together, she prepared to tell him the whole story.

He was not happy.

"She's in surgery now, if you want to come to the hospital."

"This is all your fault, you know."

She flinched at the accusation, unable to respond to his cruel words. Had she heard right?

"If you'd let her come with me today, this wouldn't have happened. Now your daughter's got a broken leg, and surgery costs a small fortune." Ever the compassionate, loving father. She fisted her free hand.

Rather than scream at him for being such an *eejit*, she shut down. Besides, the yelling tactic had never worked when they'd been married. It just made him double his belligerence. All the reasons she'd wound up asking for a divorce… "I thought you might want to come see her. I'll let you know when she's in her room." Keela hung up, her fingers trembling with anger.

Soon her eyes flooded and her face crumpled. She hated letting him get to her, but it hurt so much she could hardly breathe. Did he always have to be such an *arse*? In her gut she knew Ron would come around eventually; he always did. But never without first inflicting intentional pain. Her being his favorite target. *You've screwed up again. Why can't you be good enough, smart enough, pretty enough?*

A strong arm wrapped around her shoulders and drew her close. She buried her face in a warm neck. The full-throttle stress of the afternoon had caught up to her, and after priding herself for reasonably holding it all together—in the crying department, anyway—

she fell apart. Completely. In Daniel Delaney's arms, with Conor looking on. Several seconds later, the tsunami subsided, and she tried once again to pull it together bit by bit.

"How're you holding up?"

At first she thought Conor was asking her, which seemed odd, since she clearly wasn't holding up at all, couldn't even form words yet. Soon enough, she realized Conor's concern was for his brother.

"I'm okay, thanks," Daniel said, quietly and introspectively.

During a ragged inhalation, Keela shifted position and wondered. Was there a reason Daniel might feel uncomfortable in a hospital? But he was a doctor.

"Good. Well, listen, man, I've got to get back to work."

"Yeah. Of course," Daniel said over her head, since it was snuggled under his chin. "Thanks for checking in. We'll keep you posted."

"Take care, Keela. I'm sure Anna will be fine, and let me know if there's anything I can do."

"Thank you," she whispered, then whimpered, further embarrassing herself. But at that moment Daniel was her pillar of strength and she clung tight, grateful that he held her close.

"Call me if you need me, brother." Conor gave Daniel two firm pats on the back before he took off.

Another question popped into her head. What did Conor mean?

A moment after he left, with Daniel's warm palm rubbing her shoulder and arm, she began to calm down. And she owed Daniel an explanation. "He said it was my fault."

"What?" Daniel lifted his chin, pulling back to connect with her eyes, a crease between his brows and wearing an incredulous expression.

Gazing into the depth of his darkening green eyes, she collected herself. “He called her my daughter, like she only belongs to me.” Anger ate away at the sadness. “She’s *our* daughter. How can he be so cold?”

“That’s not right.” Daniel hugged her against his chest, and not seeing his face made it easier for her to speak her thoughts.

“I can understand him wanting to avoid me—he doesn’t love me. But Anna belongs to both of us.” More tears washed over her lids as old hurt crawled back to the surface. She’d gotten pregnant quickly, they’d had to get married, and Ron hadn’t been happy about it. Yet here he was, shacked up with the woman who’d broken up their already faltering marriage, and happy as could be about his baby son. The pain of never being able to please him twisted her insides. But that was a lost cause, so why did she let him wound her anymore? He’d broken her with so much fault-finding and heartache that she couldn’t imagine ever caring so much for *anyone* ever again. Except for her daughter. Giving her love to Ron had been one huge and messy mistake.

“The guy needs to be there for his kid. And there’s no honor in blame.” Daniel’s truthful words soothed, like light in the darkness. “No one’s responsible for this. Accidents happen. Don’t even let yourself go there.”

But she already had. Thanks to Ron, who was more than happy to show her the way.

“Hell, if it’s anyone’s fault, it’s mine,” Daniel said. “It was my idea to walk the dunes.”

“I asked if we could come.”

“You know, it’s dumb to give this another thought. That reaction from your ex was asinine, pure and simple.”

She couldn't argue about that, and soon she relaxed against Daniel's chest, grateful for his logic and, more important, for sticking up for her. She inhaled a rough breath, letting the full weight of her head settle on his shoulder, liking the way it felt. Solid.

"And furthermore, I can't imagine any man wanting to avoid you."

Of all the crazy times for a guy to say such a sweet thing. She savored it, then tucked it away. Someday she'd remember his words like a flashlight on a scary night. Her tiny smile of gratitude against his neck drew another round of big sloppy tears, promising to drench that borrowed ER scrub top.

Over the next few days, Keela didn't leave her daughter's side except to run home to shower and change. A few days after surgery, when the swelling had gone down, the orthopedic doctor finally put the official cast on and discharged Anna. Daniel was there to help with the transport. He'd also been at the hospital at least once every single day since the accident to check in. From the way Anna's eyes lit up whenever he arrived, it was clear to Keela she'd bonded with him. Though Daniel kept his distance.

"Will you sign my cast?"

"Why would you want my name?"

"You're my doctor!"

Daniel looked to be on the verge of an explanation but soon thought better of it. He grabbed the felt marker that several of the hospital staff had already used to sign their autographs.

Keela smiled, watching Daniel draw a silly face after his name, especially when it made Anna laugh. The child had been through several tough days with surgery, recovery pain, IV antibiotics and having to look at a scary, nasty scar in progress with the postsurgical open splint. Now, with the closed cast, she could go home and begin her healing process. Keela crossed her fingers that the fracture would heal straight, as the doctor intended.

"Let me help you into the wheelchair," Daniel said, transferring Anna from the bed to the awaiting chair. "I'm parked at the curb, so we'll put you in the car and get far away from this place. Oh, and the drive home may involve a stop for ice cream. What do you say?" He seemed to be going out of his way to make her daughter happy.

"Yay!" Anna clapped her hands, obviously thrilled at going home by way of the ice cream parlor.

Ron had come for a visit, as Keela knew he would, but he'd seemed like he wanted to leave the instant he arrived. Though she did give him a nod for bringing his daughter a teddy bear with a broken leg, and for giving her some DVDs of her favorite animated movies to help pass the time in the hospital. He'd even offered Keela an apology of sorts for his blunt behavior on the phone the night of the accident. "I was a little harsh the other night, but it was because I was worried."

Whatever. Damage done.

Keela gathered the few items Anna had at the hospital and put them in the large plastic discharge bag the nurse had left. "I'm ready. Are you?"

"Yes!" Even a nasty leg break and a clunky cast couldn't dampen Anna's natural enthusiasm. The child never ceased to amaze her.

They arrived home Thursday afternoon within the hour, with fresh ice cream drips on Anna's top and skirt. Daniel helped deliver the patient to the living room couch.

"Anything I can get for you before I leave?"

"Don't leave. *Please...?*" Anna whined.

He looked confused at the way she had attached herself to him. "But I've got patients to see at the clinic. I promise to come to see you tomorrow, okay?"

Uncharacteristically, Anna pouted, folding her arms and pushing out her lower lip. A big act, of course, and Daniel was most likely onto her. But being the good guy he was, he played along.

"Should I have my patients come here so I won't have to leave?" He got out his cell phone, pretending to be ready to place his call.

"Yes." With arms still crossed, she gave one affirmative nod.

Daniel glanced to Keela for help.

She shook her head and nearly laughed at his help-a-guy-out expression. "I have an idea. Why don't you come back for dinner?" she said, not even sure she had enough food in the house to make a proper meal.

"Yay!" Anna worked the sick-kid angle to the limit.

"I've got a better idea," Daniel said. "I'll bring dinner when I come back. You have enough to do without cooking for me. Deal?"

There was much appealing about Daniel Delaney, but his consideration for others was one of the strongest draws. "Since I'm wrecked, I won't fight you on that," she said gratefully. Sleeping on the pullout chair in the hospital room for the past several days, with all the interruptions, had proved to be challenging. She looked forward to a long shower and maybe even a nap, if she could get Anna settled. The last thing she wanted to do was cook dinner.

"Deal. See you later." He headed for the door. "Be good, Anna."

One glance at Anna, beaming from the couch, and Keela recognized that look. The child had a serious crush going on.

Keela didn't have a clue how to deal with that right at the moment, since she could totally relate. Confused and exhausted as she was, she admitted she had a crush on Daniel, too.

When he came back that evening, Daniel's earlier enthusiasm was absent. All Keela sensed was obligation. She hated how that felt. Sure, he put on a happy face for Anna and was cordial, maybe even a little sweet with Keela—like when he insisted on serving their dinner like a waiter, wearing a towel over his arm. But the minute Anna went to bed, he was out of there.

"I need to take a run before I turn in tonight," he said. "It's been a long day, and the only thing that helps me settle down is jogging."

Before he left, he asked if there was anything she needed, and insisted she call if she thought of something later. Then he promised to help out any way he could—again the obligation for being a hero—and literally took off running from her porch.

What had happened to the guy who'd said he couldn't imagine any man avoiding her?

Daniel wasn't prepared for how hard it was to spend time with Keela outside of work. Or how easy it had been for little Anna to squirm into his heart. Being around them while in the hospital had been a completely different experience. He was a visitor, in and out. Tonight, at Keela's, he was a guest, a very welcomed guest, and Anna treated him like he was the greatest guy on the planet. Truth was he enjoyed that part, Anna's admiration, even though it tugged at dreams he'd had to let go of after Emma had died. Made him think what age she'd be now, or if she'd be anything like Anna. He couldn't go there, wasn't ready. It was still too upsetting.

Plus the gratitude he saw in Keela's eyes when he'd brought dinner shook him up. He could get used to staring into those clear blues if he wasn't careful.

He wasn't ready to go there, either. Especially not with an employee.

So he'd faked his way through dinner, bringing takeout cartons from the Drumcliffe restaurant, filled with a little something for everyone.

Keela had to be sick of hospital food, so he'd brought a chicken and wild rice dish with garden vegetables for her. Rita, the hotel chef, made the best mac and cheese in town, too. What kid didn't love that? Anna had wolfed it down like her cast was hollow.

The food hadn't been the issue, though. It was how tempting it felt to be there, in their home, away from the safe clinic.

Being brutally honest, he wanted more. The realization had sent him running out the door, unsure when, if ever, he'd go back.

Over the next few days, all Anna talked about was Daniel and all the nice things he'd done for her. He even called her once a day from work just to see how she was doing. What man did that? Not Anna's own father, that was for sure.

Keela had to admit all the talk about Daniel this and Daniel that was getting on her nerves, since she was trying her best to resist falling for the guy. But how could a mother resist a man who'd saved her kid? A man who'd let her cry on his shoulder, and who'd stuck up for her? A man who insisted on her staying off work, with pay? Though she did wonder how he was managing without her.

Easy. She had to be honest, keep her feet grounded. Number one, he was her boss. She couldn't dare let a little crush jeopardize her job. She needed to work to get by. Number two, she was still hurting from the divorce. Sure, it had been a year and a half, but she needed longer to heal. Ron's emotionally abusive behavior had cut her to the core. Number three, she couldn't trust her judgment in men. Hadn't she thought Ron was the love of her life when she'd met and married him? Anna's dad would forever be living proof that Keela made bad choices where men were concerned. She couldn't trust herself when it came to picking them. Not even good guys like Daniel Delaney.

The quick thoughts, as she cleaned her small house while Anna napped, helped her realize she was beginning to adjust her attitude a bit. She'd just thought of Ron as Anna's dad, not her ex-husband. Maybe that was the initial step in moving on from the devastating divorce. She hoped so, anyway.

There was something else to consider, which hadn't gone unnoticed. Though Daniel had been standoffish with Anna at first, after he'd saved her much had changed. Their friendship wasn't exactly easy-peasy, but the visible tension Keela had seen the first day he'd watched Anna had leveled off some. These days, he even teased her and played along with her games. But now the guy seemed totally uncomfortable when it was just him and Keela alone. Except for when they'd waited during surgery. He'd opened up to her just a little then, but now he'd clamped back down. All business.

She could have all the fanciful feelings she wanted for the man, but blatant one-sided attraction was a waste of time. Who needed the frustration?

Truth was, Keela missed the way it used to be at work, where they both had their set jobs. This going off script with visits to her house and quiet dinners, just the three of them, had confused her and thrown a wrench into their boss-employee dynamic.

For the sake of survival, she'd have to break her daughter's heart and put things back the way they used to be. Keela needed to go back to work. ASAP.

She searched for her cell phone. "Daniel? It's Keela."

"Is everything all right with Anna?"

"Oh, yeah, she's great. I'm calling about me."

"Are you okay?"

Not really. "I'm fine. I'm calling because I'd like to come back to work."

"No, no, no. You take as much time off as you need. You've got to look after Anna while she heals."

"She's coming along great, she's nearly mastered walking with crutches and Mrs. Jenkins said she'd come to our house if that worked better for a while."

"Nope, both you and Anna are better off with your being there while she gets better."

"That's a bit thick, don't you think?"

"Thick?"

"Unfair. What about my patients? What about the college athletes?"

"I've got a registry PT filling in. He can't compare to you, but we're getting by."

She cringed inwardly over the possibility of someone stepping into her shoes at work and eventually walking off with them *and* her job. Plus Daniel had kept that bit of information to himself until just now. Why? Well, *stuff* pride. "I need my job, Daniel."

"I know you do. Don't worry about that. Right now you deserve paid time off."

His benevolence was beginning to get under her skin. "I'd rather work, thanks."

"Why not wait until Anna is completely confident on crutches and further along with healing. You're a PT. You can start working with her on strengthening exercises. She's a quick learner. It won't be long. If you're worried about your job, don't be. I'm saving it for you. I'd be nuts not to."

How could she protest?

Daniel sat in his office, mindlessly staring at his computer screen. He missed Keela and, hard as it was to believe, Anna, but the fallout from being around them was too great. Every step he took toward Keela carried the consequence of bitter and painful memories of Kathryn walking away. Of loving someone more than she could ever possibly love him. Of being blind to the fact there had been nothing he could've done to change her feelings.

Since Anna's accident, the onslaught of thoughts of Emma, tiny and helpless, had been relentless. Over the past year, Daniel had worked hard to get past the daily memories, and he'd made progress before Anna had skipped into his life. Now he seemed to be back at square one of the healing game.

He'd wanted to be a father, Emma's father, more than he could have ever imagined. Though she'd been lifeless in his arms, his heart had instantaneously bonded with her. He could hardly bear reliving those moments, yet they'd returned again and again when he least expected. How many times could a man replay the saddest moment of his life without breaking apart?

He'd thought he'd made good strides on his road to emotional recovery until he'd let his guard down and looked at Keela romantically. If venturing into uncharted territory with someone new meant getting shredded by the past, he simply wasn't ready to go there. No matter how appealing Keela and her daughter were.

It had been a week since he'd seen them, and several days since he'd insisted Keela not come back to work. Sure, he could have used her help, but for now he needed to keep her out of his daily life. To get back on track. The 4Cs athletes were officially beginning to filter through his clinic. Every single one of his appointment slots had been booked, a huge boost to the business. Some double booked. Since he didn't have Keela's help, he'd hired a PT assistant from a temporary agency instead. He had to keep the college happy, and that meant being focused. Working with Keela right now would guarantee distraction. Sure, he felt bad that he hadn't made time to visit Anna or even call to say hi lately, but he was functioning in survival mode these days.

Anna deserved better, and so did Keela. *Not so fast, buddy. Your motives weren't that pure.* He'd also cut back on visits because he couldn't get the disturbing memory out of his mind of having Keela's warm body tucked close to his. The quick sensual thought sent a shiver through his chest. That was the real reason he'd insisted she take more time off work—to keep distance between them.

"Dr. Delaney?" Phil, the temporary PT, appeared at his door. "We're out of pain-relieving gel and I just used the last package of electrode pads for the electronic muscle stimulator."

Did you think to order any the way I showed you last week? "I'll call the supply company and put in an order stat. Anything else we're low on?"

Phil verbally tossed several more items his way, and Daniel gritted his teeth while writing them down.

The fill-in registry guy was doing an adequate job, but his communication skills weren't great. And he didn't know squat about ordering supplies. And he definitely didn't look as good as Keela in the clinic uniform.

Truth was, Keela had spoiled Daniel. Over the past three months, they'd quickly gotten their work routine down, and sometimes it seemed she was a mind reader. He'd grown lazy, never having to be explicit about what he wanted or needed her to do for a patient. Often her input or ideas were better than his own care plans. But that was neither here nor there because he'd essentially banished her from work for another week.

He needed time to figure this out, to separate his misplaced desire from reality, since pain and heartache came with opening up and letting someone in. Besides, he had no business further confusing the affections of a daddy-starved little girl and preying on her vulnerable mother because he had a crush. Hell, that would make him ten times worse than the deadbeat dad!

Daniel grimaced, seeing himself in such a dim light. On one hand he wanted to take a chance again. On the other hand, the hurting side, he was still running scared. Why be a moth to a flame?

Good thing he had appointments up the wazoo and didn't have another second to think about Keela. Here he wore the mask of a doctor running his own clinic with confidence, even though inside much still needed to be put back together. And he'd thought he'd made progress. *Sure, guy.*

The intercom buzzed "Your next patient's in room two."

Grateful for the distraction, he shot out of his swivel chair, heading for the office door.

Keela had too much time on her hands. Anna was already a dynamo on her crutches, and their tiny house had been cleaned within an inch of its life. How many times could they watch the latest animated movies together and not go stir-crazy?

She also missed Daniel, the good boss turned superhero.

Lately she'd even started an unwise game of listing all the ways he was different from Ron. Stable, dependable, trustworthy, loyal, kind, sweet. Sexy as hell. Seeing him shirtless had ended any questions about that.

She blew the hair out of her eyes from bending over the bathroom tile, scrubbing the ugly pink grout within an inch of its chipping and cracking life. She needed to go back to work. Didn't he get that about her?

Why let some temporary PT assistant treat the patients when she knew the job backward and forward? Did the guy know where they kept the second TENS machine? Was he keeping the supply cabinet stocked? Did he even know how to order from their vendors? The place was probably falling apart without her. Yet Daniel wouldn't let her come back.

Maybe if he saw how much better Anna was, and how

desperate Keela was to get back on the job, he'd change his mind about her staying off work another week.

On her knees, she pulled off the thick yellow rubber gloves and tugged her cell phone out of her jeans' rear pocket to make the call. "Hi, Daniel." Her voice echoed off the bathroom walls.

Admittedly, he sounded surprised and maybe a little hesitant.

"Anna's doing great, thanks." She fiddled with her hair, as if they might be doing FaceTime and she hadn't thought to comb it. "So, I know you must be crazy-mad busy these days, and probably skipping meals to keep up, so, uh, well, here's the story. You're Anna's hero, and I'd like to invite you for dinner Saturday night. The reason I'm saying Saturday is because I know the clinic's closed and you might have some extra time on your hands. Of course, who knows, since I've been off work, maybe you've changed the schedule and added weekend appointments to keep up with all the new 4Cs patients. But of course you still wouldn't work Saturday evenings, now, would you? So anyway, I thought you might appreciate a home-cooked meal at O'Mara's pub." She caught her breath and waited for an answer, fearing the line had gone dead.

"I would have said yes about ten minutes ago, but you wouldn't stop talking." He sounded subdued for the pushy boss she knew, but she skimmed over it.

She slumped against the cold, pink-tiled wall, wearing a well-earned grin. "Great. Is six okay? Anna likes to eat early."

"Sure." Again, he didn't exactly sound enthusiastic, just willing. "Tell her I said hello." Ah, there was the guy she remembered and missed, the one who worried about her daughter. "I'm sorry I haven't been by." Why did it feel like years since they'd seen each other?

"I understand. And will do on the saying-hi part. Do you eat lamb?" She stood and stared at herself in the bathroom mirror, then cringed at how bad her hair looked.

"Sure. Doesn't everyone?"

How could a single phrase make her feel giddy? The man was so Irish. "I'm thinking of making my famous stew." Gathering confidence, she smiled at herself in the mirror and fiddled with her hair again, tucking one side behind her ear and fluffing the other side. Her stew was anything but famous. Ron had reminded her of that often enough—along with the rest of her cooking. But what did Daniel know? The guy ate lamb!

"I'm hungry already." He sounded a bit distracted, probably multitasking, but he was saying all the right things—she'd give him that.

"Great. Can't wait to see you!" *Oops, that slipped out.*

The phone went quiet, and Keela wondered if by any chance Daniel was sitting at his desk with the same dreamy grin on his face as she had on hers.

As dangerous as that would be…she sure hoped so.

"Me, too."

After accepting her invitation and saying goodbye, Daniel hung up the desk phone and sat staring at it. He'd heard the smile in Keela's voice, felt her need to be around grown-ups—just him, or would anyone do?—and he dreaded being the one she'd called. He couldn't very well avoid her forever, but Saturday felt awfully close.

Moth to flame. The image set in.

At least he had a few days to prepare. She might think of him as a hero…well, so be it, because he intended to show up on Saturday night wearing full body armor.

Chapter Four

Saturday, Daniel knocked on Keela's front door at 5:30 p.m., then glanced through the fan-shaped glazed glass portion. He'd given himself three different versions of the proverbial pep talk on the short drive over. *First, don't make more out of this than it is. It's dinner with an employee and her daughter. Second, everything doesn't have to be a torture test. Third, relax and enjoy yourself.* Yet he still tensed beneath the firmly placed body armor.

Muffled sounds and activity came from inside the cottage as he waited, leaning a hand on the door, watching through the front window. Moving like an Olympic champion in the crutch-walking competition, Anna sprinted for the gold to open the door. "Mommy's drowning!"

"What?" He bolted around Anna into the tiny living room and toward the kitchen, where squeals and familiar Irish curses came. "Swearing a hole in a pot," as his grandfather would phrase it.

"Blast you!" Keela growled while wrestling with the kitchen faucet, which had turned into Old Faithful, spouting an arching flow into the air, across the counter, and creating a small waterfall onto the floor.

"Move over so I can get under the sink and turn off the water," he said, dropping a small bouquet of flowers onto a dry section of her counter. He nudged a drenched Keela aside to open the cupboards, then dived inside. Water splattered onto his back as he did, sending chills up his neck. Not wasting any time, he found the pipe handles and twisted them clockwise. The geyser stopped. He pulled his head out, catching counter overflow in his hair as he did, then looked up at Keela, who was dripping wet and wild-eyed.

"The faucet leak got worse and I tried to turn the handle extra tight to stop it and..." She held the fixture that had come off and stared at it in wonderment.

"Do you have a wrench?" He shook water from his hair before it could run into his eyes.

"No." She bit her lip.

He made a quick study of her setup and decided what he'd most likely need to fix it. Having been raised at the family hotel, all three Delaney boys knew how to do minor and sometimes major repairs, though Mark was by far the best. "Let me run home and get some tools and stuff. Be right back."

"Can I come with you?" Anna asked, as if afraid to be left behind with her half-crazed mother in the semi-flooded kitchen.

"Anna," Keela said, snapping out of shock and directly into mom mode, "I need you to help me mop up this mess." She glanced at her soaked shirt. "Ack, I've got to change my clothes, too."

"Be back in five," he said, dashing to the front door. Then, remembering the bouquet he'd brought, he added, "Oh, those flowers are for you." And off he went.

True to his word, he was back and fixing the sink faucet in short order, having given Keela a chance to get out of her sopping clothes. She'd put on a cap-sleeved camellia-pink top and another pair of jeans, which he had to say fit great. Though her hair was still dripping wet, as if she'd just come straight from a shower. A quick thought of her *in* that shower threw him, so he glanced toward the sink, avoiding her eyes.

"I need to blow-dry my hair, if you don't mind."

"No problem. I'll get to work on this." He was thankful for the distraction.

Anna stuck by his side, watching his every move with fascination. At first it made him uncomfortable, having her wanting to be near him. It occurred to him he hadn't thought about Emma today, and he felt guilty. But Anna wasn't Emma, and she didn't deserve to be ignored, so every once in a while he forced a glance at her adoring face and tried to smile. It didn't come easy but the second time, surprising himself, he winked. The huge, encouraging grin she gave in return nearly melted his heart. *May as well talk to her, since she isn't going away.*

"So what's new?" he asked while using the wrench and trying to distract her laser stare.

"Nothin'."

"Nothing? What've you been up to?"

"I don't know."

The kid had obviously developed a bad case of cabin fever. Or forgetfulness. "Well, we'll have to do something about that."

"What's that?" she asked, pointing.

"That's a seat washer. And this is plumber's grease. See how I do it?" He coated the replacement washer with the stuff before installing it.

"Wow."

Yeah, heck with that guy selling imported beer on that commercial; he'd just officially become the most *interesting* man in the world. Granted, it was a very small world—Anna's world—but he'd take the title, since she so openly offered it, and the thought put a smile on his face. Maybe, with some practice, he'd get used to being around this little girl.

It also occurred to him, as he finished the kitchen repair and cleaned up the counter, that living in an old cottage like this, Keela probably had other sinks in need of new rings and rubber washers, and since he was in the neighborhood…

"I'm done in here," he called out. "You want me to look at your bathroom faucets, too?"

She waltzed back into the kitchen, her golden-tipped, light brown hair down and brushing her shoulders, and those amazing eyes lined with makeup, looking fantastic. The sight nearly stopped his train of thought.

"Could you, please? They're leaking, too."

Nothing like feeling needed by a great-looking woman. "I've got my tool kit, and there's no time like the present," he said, suddenly feeling extra manly.

"Well, I'm a bit behind with dinner now, so if you really don't mind…"

"Not at all. Just point me to the bathroom."

"I'll show you!" Anna said, leading the way on her lightweight titanium crutches for the "most interesting man in the world," making another chink in his faulty armor.

* * *

Keela dashed around in the kitchen, wiping up the remaining water and trying to get a hold on her nerves. She hadn't cooked for a man since she'd divorced Ron. All she could hope was that Daniel wasn't as hard to please.

It occurred to her that when she'd first met Ron, he'd thought everything she did was great. He'd loved her cooking, but over time he became pickier and pickier. Too much this or not enough that. Why couldn't she learn some Italian-American dishes, his nationality? he'd chide. In the last year of their marriage, meals had become the tensest time of her day.

She fussed with the stew gravy, taking a sip, worrying she hadn't added enough salt or Worcestershire sauce. Had she put too much Guinness in it? *Stop this. Daniel isn't Ron.*

Picking up the pieces of her remaining self-esteem, she made a promise to serve her specialty with pride, not worry. Food always tasted better that way.

Twenty minutes later, after he'd fixed the slow drip in the bathroom sink, enticing aromas from the kitchen and a hungry growl in Daniel's stomach lured him out of the bathroom. His shadow followed right behind. Anna had been so quiet, he'd almost forgotten she was there.

"Should be good to go now."

"I can't thank you enough," Keela said, putting the finishing touches on setting the small kitchen table, his bouquet of slightly wet flowers at the center, then transferring the pot of stew to a trivet next to the vase.

"You already are. Dinner smells great." He especially liked how she looked standing in her small kitchen, mismatched potholders for gloves. So different from the work uniform and patient-care Keela he was used to. It surprised him how grateful she looked at his compliment.

"I hope you like it. Stew is a staple, or I should say, was a staple back home."

"My grandda will be envious."

She blushed, and the pink on her cheeks stopped Daniel cold. Not being around her at work for the past few weeks, he'd forgotten how lovely her eyes were, and how ivory her skin. She nodded toward the seat at the head of the table for him to sit. He did, but not without being aware of the honor, and not sure he deserved it. He waited for Keela and Anna to take their seats.

Soon, they all enjoyed a surprisingly good meal together. Surprising, because he'd grown up eating his grandfather's stew and couldn't imagine anything being as good.

"So, tell me what's been going on at work," Keela said eagerly while dipping a homemade biscuit into some lamb stew gravy.

He filled her in, in between delicious mouthfuls, on the new college account with the never-ending flow of young athletes through the clinic doors. Falling back on the comfort of their usual relationship made dinner at her house easier to navigate, especially with Anna's big eyes watching his every move.

Pride over the clinic stretched his smile as he brought Keela up to date, particularly when he realized how impressed she was. Now he had two adoring sets of eyes watching him. As they ate and talked, he sensed how anxious Keela was to come back. She'd said as much in their previous phone call.

Daniel also couldn't help but notice how eager to please Anna was, passing the biscuits without being asked, then the butter, then the jam. Not butting in to the "grown-ups" conversation. Well, not always. He could tell by the subtle expressions from Keela that this wasn't usual behavior, especially Anna cleaning her plate. Was she doing it because he was their guest, or had she been trained to try extra hard to make her daddy happy?

"That's a first," Keela teased.

"It's good, Mommy."

"Ah, thanks, sweetie."

"She's right. Delicious. And if you don't mind, I'll have seconds. My grandfather swears he makes the best stew in the world, probably due to the generous dashes of Guinness." Daniel hadn't expected anything to come close from Keela, but he'd been gratefully surprised. "I'm not so sure now."

Him asking for seconds changed Keela's tentative hostess demeanor to confident cook. That alone was worth the effort he'd made to socialize with his attractive employee. After a few bites, he'd quickly figured out it was the company that made the good meal special. That secret ingredient couldn't be replaced with stout.

When they finished eating, as he helped clear the table, Keela hesitated before turning on the faucet.

"Hey, let me help with the dishes," he insisted, showing off his handiwork and filling the sink with warm water, noting subtle relief in her expression.

"Can I dry?" Anna asked.

Keela pulled in her chin and blinked at the mystery child.

"Another first?" Daniel murmured.

"Usually I have to twist her arm."

The dinner cleanup turned into a team sport, adding another chink to his armor, and soon the kitchen was spotless.

"I'll make some coffee if you'd like, and I've got a little something for dessert."

"Coffee sounds good. Dessert maybe later?" He patted his completely satisfied stomach.

"Come play with me, Dr. Daniel." Anna tugged on his hand. She couldn't possibly know how she tortured him with her innocent pleas, reminding him of all the activities he'd never get to do with his baby girl.

Needing to show progress in his mourning, he stopped Keela before she could protest. "What do you want to play?"

"I'll show you. Come on." Anna led the way, and, though reluctantly, he followed.

Keela gave him a grateful glance and went to work making coffee, and it occurred to him that being here had been easier than he'd expected. He figured the third point in his pep talk had sunk in—relax and enjoy yourself. Maybe being around the kid would act like a vaccine, and soon he'd have immunity and she'd cease to be a trigger for missing Emma. On the other hand, facing time alone with the mom would take a lot more effort.

By the time Keela had put the cherry pie into the oven to warm for later and made the coffee, Anna and Daniel had finished their first game of Match. Anna being the decisive winner, she hooted to prove it. Keela would have a little talk with her about good sportsmanship tomorrow.

She placed two cups and saucers on the coffee table and watched the two of them play. It didn't take long to catch on that Daniel was letting Anna win. Over and over. And Anna was eating up both the attention and her victories.

She thrust her hands into the air after her third win. "Yay! I'm pretty good at this, huh?"

"You sure are." He took a sip from his coffee and from over the cup winked at Keela.

That was a first! She smiled, warmth rambling around in her chest for her boss and her daughter. No way could she deny what a good man he was, or how much she'd enjoyed his company tonight. Not to mention how he'd saved the day, again, by fixing her faucets. And how amazing he was with Anna. Yeah, he was definitely a great guy. And he liked her cooking.

But taking a sip of her coffee, it occurred to her—that was what she'd thought about Ron at first, too.

Anna argued when Keela suggested it was time for bed. "I want Dr. Daniel to read to me."

Not what he'd signed up for. The thought of reading to Anna sent a shot of dread through him.

"He's our guest, sweetie. I'll read."

Anna squirmed and fussed. *What harm could it do? A helluva lot!* But the kid had been on near house arrest since having her traumatizing accident. Being the adult, shouldn't he put her wants before his need to avoid her? "That's okay, I'll read her a story."

Beaming and suddenly once again Little Miss Cooperation, Anna chose one of her huge collection of Curious George stories, and to make a tough job even more difficult, she rested her head on his arm as he read. Her blatant affection for him, plus the little-girl shampoo scent, set off a rogue wave of sadness. He distractedly massaged his breast bone, unsure if he was trying to rub away the memories or just survive the moment. By the end of George's adventure, Anna's eyes had closed and her head nodded forward. So innocent. So vulnerable.

He rubbed at that sensation behind his sternum again, then laid her back on the pillow, covered and tucked her in. After tiptoeing to the door, he whispered for Keela to come and say good-night.

The tender look she gave him just before entering her daughter's room danced circles around that weird feeling in his chest. Which made him tense up, and soon anxiety replaced the warm and fuzzy feeling. This wasn't his kid and Keela was his employee. What the hell was he doing here?

Later, after he'd replayed his pep talk to no avail, they sat and chatted in her cozy living room, mostly more about work and the various physical problems the jocks had, a safe and boring topic that allowed his mind to wander. Out of the blue he fought the urge to kiss her. He'd sat too close, her shampoo smelled nothing like her daughter's and the trace of vanilla set off a desire he'd pushed under since holding her in the ER the night of Anna's accident. The need came out of nowhere but planted temptation deep and strong. Should he? Wouldn't it mess everything up with their boss-employee situation?

Letting his natural instinct take over by kissing her would only complicate things. And it would open a mystery box of problems. None of which he could think of at the moment, because all he wanted to do was kiss those lips he couldn't stop watching. He understood the ramifications would be far reaching, and most likely painful. He lifted his eyes, only then realizing she knew where his gaze had settled. He saw the welcoming spark as she looked at him, then quickly away, probably wondering if he'd made up his mind. Well? Was he going to kiss her or not?

"Would you like to share some wine with me? I have a really good pinot noir."

Her invitation to stick around and let down his guard, though obvious, considerate and very tempting, only made him more tense. This wasn't a good idea, relaxing, kissing. *Remember how Kathryn shredded your heart.* Plus it was bad form kissing an employee, bad for business and any future dealings at work. What if he'd misread her invitation and she didn't want him to kiss her? Every negative thought proved one thing: he wasn't ready to take this step. So even though it wasn't yet 9:00 p.m., he came up with a lame excuse to leave.

"That sounds great, but I've really been missing in action for Daisy lately, and I promised to walk her tonight when I got home." It wasn't a blatant lie—he'd actually thought about it earlier, on the drive over, hoping the dinner would be short and sweet. And merely an obligation. All business. No pleasure. But nothing had turned out the way he'd expected, starting with his dramatic entrance, a fantastic dinner, and ending with reading a bedtime story and the offer of a grown-up beverage from an incredibly attractive woman.

He was probably the biggest fool on the planet, but he glanced at his watch. "It's already later than I realized." He saw the flash of disappointment in her brilliant blues—since she'd just offered him some wine and who knew what else?—but he wasn't ready to find out what kissing her would be like. Not yet. And he knew if he stuck around and drank wine with her, he would kiss her. And that would change everything. "Another time?"

She nodded benevolently, though he sensed her letdown. "I can't thank you enough for fixing my faucets."

"Hey, no problem. Anytime you need help, just let me know." Like that, they shifted back to business mode. Then, like an idiot who evidently still wasn't ready to move on, he left without even a quick buss of her cheek. Or thanking her again for the great meal, and even better company. So intent on getting out of there fast, he didn't even hug her good-night.

Damn, he was out of practice.

True to his word, he walked Daisy on the beach as soon as he got home. Then and only then did he try to put everything into perspective. He'd been swept up into the world of Keela and Anna since the accident. Try as he may to resist them, he kept finding reasons to go back. He'd offered to help whenever she needed it, too. Was he acting like a fool or a guy who saw something in a woman he'd like to find out more about?

He'd always have to deal with the pain of losing Emma, and the woman he'd wanted to marry walking away, but maybe it was time to separate *that* from Keela and Anna. They weren't responsible for his broken heart in any way. If he got honest with himself and removed the blinders, he might see clearly the great woman in front of him. She was easy on the eyes, loved her daughter and was a good cook and a total pleasure to be around. Did he need to get hit over the head to figure out that was enough?

Keela was a no-drama kind of lady, nothing like Kathryn, and that was the part he liked best. He couldn't deny how relaxed he'd felt at dinner, and it'd gotten easier to be around Anna. Everything had gone well up until the point of wanting to kiss Keela. Before that, he hadn't thought or worried about the clinic, until she'd asked, and only then wondering how he could go on holding things together with the registry PT, when the person he needed to help the clinic stay afloat was Keela.

He needed her on so many levels it took the wind out of him, or had Daisy sped up the walk? An anxious pang lodged in Daniel's chest, the same old anger and hurt that kept dragging him down. He needed to face the fact that he was interested in Keela and deal with it, not run away. Interest didn't equal love. It was *just* interest. Hell, he hadn't even kissed her yet!

The problem was, what if that interest turned into want, or need? He never intended to be in a position of wanting someone more than they wanted him again.

"Daisy, I'm a mess," he said, beginning a jog to keep up with his dog. She whined and yipped and pulled the leash and him toward the edge of the water.

The following Friday, Keela still replayed the moment she could have sworn Daniel Delaney wanted to kiss her. She'd been so positive he would that she'd lightly licked her lips in preparation. Then, as if a heavy curtain had dropped between them, he'd backed away. She'd hoped to get him to stick around and relax with some wine; maybe then he'd feel comfortable enough to open up. To kiss her? Heck, after a glass of wine, she might have been the one to initiate that kiss. Who knew? Because he'd ducked out on her, quickly, and she was still trying to figure out what she could have done differently. Maybe she was just the kind of girl men ducked out on. Ron certainly had.

Her phone rang, and after not hearing from Daniel all week, she let her hopes fly. But it was a woman's voice on the other end of the line.

"Keela, this is Maureen Delaney."

They shared a couple seconds of niceties as Keela's hope dwindled but her curiosity rose.

"I'm sorry to call on such short notice, but I just had

two hotel guests ask about spa treatments for tomorrow. I've lined up the esthetician, but they both said they also wanted a massage. Is there any way you're available?"

Still going stir-crazy from not working, Keela wanted to leap at this chance to get out of the house and use her old skills, not to mention to earn some extra money. But she had Anna to think about and Mrs. Jenkins had told her she'd be gone all weekend. "If I can find childcare, I should be able to."

"Oh, right. I know I said I could watch Anna for you when we first spoke about your taking this job, but tomorrow we have a busload of quilters checking in right around the time the other guests made those spa appointments."

Desperate not to let the new opportunity slip by, Keela thought of Daniel. Hadn't he said something to the effect about anytime she needed help to call him? He hadn't appreciated the last-minute childcare duties at work that day, but that was before he and Anna had been through so much together. He didn't seem to mind reading her a book last Saturday night, either. Wouldn't Keela be helping his mother and the family business at The Drumcliffe Hotel?

"Let me make a call and get right back to you."

She hung up the landline and fished out the cell phone from her purse. Her boss was in her top five contacts, for purely business reasons, she rationalized, so she speed-dialed him. "Hi, Daniel, it's Keela."

He sounded happy to hear from her, which made her smile and boosted her confidence, so they chatted briefly before she got to the point. "So your mother has asked me to work tomorrow afternoon and I'm desperate for childcare. Mrs. Jenkins left this morning to visit her sister in Pismo Beach, and—"

"If you don't mind her hanging out at the clinic with me for a while," he said, breaking into her long-winded explanation, "I can watch her. How long are we talking?"

He'd offered? Wow. "I've got two appointments, so at least a couple of hours." Her head spun with things she'd need to prepare today, like scented candles, body oils and creams. And music! Where had she put her new age and nature sounds CDs? Had she uploaded any into her phone? So busy thinking, she didn't hear his answer. "What?"

"I said sure. Bring her by the clinic on your way to the hotel."

There he was, saving the day. Again. "Perfect. Thank you!"

Late Saturday afternoon, Daniel finished up some paperwork and patient chart entries. Unlike the first time he'd watched Anna in the clinic, this time she sat quietly coloring. Maybe the huge and heavy cast had something to do with it, but he suspected it had more to do with her wanting to be good for him. He'd promised the sooner he got done, the sooner they could go to the beach. Also, unlike the first time in his office, he noticed it was easier to be around her. His theory on developing immunity seemed to be panning out.

"Okay, squirt, I'm done. You still wanna go to the beach?"

She quickly finished with the yellow crayon. "Yes!"

"I suppose you want some ice cream first?"

She clapped.

He shut down the computer, then helped pick up all the discarded coloring book pages, stuffing them into her backpack until she stopped him. "This one's for you."

She handed him a picture of a smiling little girl with a bouquet of flowers. Some of it had started out neat and between the lines, but the rest was a wild and furious mess of crayon scribbles. “For me? Thank you. Is that you?” She’d colored the little girl’s hair brown.

“Yes. I’m giving you flowers for watching me so Mommy could work.”

“Hey, that’s nice.” He took the page and pinned it to the corkboard on which he kept important notices and memos. It was definitely getting easier to be around her.

“She has a fever.”

He handed her the crutches after helping her put the backpack on. “The little girl in the picture?”

“No, Mommy.”

“She’s sick?” And working at the hotel?

“She says cabin fever.”

He laughed. “I see.” Keela hadn’t been kidding when she’d said she wanted to come back to work. Well, his schedule showed she was due back on Monday, and though he’d given the substitute PT notice, he’d decided to have them overlap for her first week back. Business at the clinic had really picked up and it’d been several weeks since Keela had worked. The extra hands could only be a good thing until she got back into the swing of their routine.

Daniel grabbed his cell phone and texted Keela. Heading to the beach by the hotel. Meet us when you can.

“Let’s get that ice cream now.”

Keela finished her back-to-back massages on a high, even though her muscles ached. She’d forgotten how much she enjoyed helping people relax, smoothing away the tightness in their muscles. Not to mention the side benefits of enjoying the aroma therapy and peaceful music. She'd also forgotten how much upper body strength the job required, using not just her hands but her forearms and elbows, too. Both clients had also tipped her generously, on top of the check Maureen had just cut for her.

Being inside the hotel reminded her of when she'd first stayed there six years ago. Quaint, clean, quiet. Spacious enough rooms, though slightly outdated… Still, she could set up her massage table and have plenty of space to maneuver. A full-body massage required a lot of elbow room. This time, she'd come to the hotel in an official capacity, as a hired massage therapist. Boy, had times changed.

She seemed to float out to her car in the parking lot, only then seeing the text from Daniel, which made her good-mood smile stretch wider. She looked up and out toward the ocean and caught a glimpse of them on the beach. The sight enveloped her with a happy, warm feeling.

After putting her supplies in the car, she took off the masseuse smock. Her sleeveless V-neck, white cotton shell was fine for the beach, but she decided to roll the yoga pants up to her knees and kick off her slip-on shoes. Then, barefoot, she took off at a quick clip across the sand.

She caught up to them at the shoreline. Daniel held Anna piggyback style, her cast sticking out like a neon-pink fiberglass ramrod as he challenged the waves licking the sand. Anna giggled and squealed as Daniel bobbed and weaved amid the waves. They both grinned and laughed as he got wetter and wetter, finally daring to wade out up to his knees, yet still protecting her cast from the water.

"Hey, you two, quit having so much fun," she called out from a dozen feet away.

Daniel turned, his childlike expression taking her by surprise. Cutting loose with her daughter only made him more appealing, and she wasn't sure what to do about that, since he apparently wasn't as interested as she was.

She ran toward them, dipped her hands in the water, then splashed it their way. Anna screamed with delight when the cold water splattered across her arms and back. Daniel lunged toward Keela and kicked wave water her way. She jumped back to avoid it, lost her balance and went down on one knee in time for another incoming wave, getting hit by buckets of cold water.

Anna and Daniel laughed.

"Ahh! Now you asked for it." Scrambling to her feet,, she scooped up more water, careful to fling it Daniel's way, because of Anna's cast. "Hey, no fair, my hands are tied."

She laughed wickedly and scooped more and more, getting closer each time until she'd gotten both of their backs as wet as hers. A huge wave crashed and nearly took all of them down before they retreated. Keela stopped for an instant, worried sick she might have ruined the supposedly waterproof cast, which hadn't been tested yet. She glanced at her daughter, who looked happier than she'd seen her in ages. Keela soon realized she hadn't had this much fun frolicking at the beach since she'd been a kid.

Out of breath and drenched, she stood at a safe distance, her hands raised. "I call a truce."

"It's a good thing, too, because Anna and I were about to dunk you good."

"Oh, right, like you could."

"Is that a dare?"

Daniel wore shades, so she couldn't see his eyes, but everything about him said he wasn't through playing yet. On impulse, she tore off up the beach, and he chased her. And damn, it felt great.

"Anna, you're supposed to be on my side," she called over her shoulder. "Make him stop!"

Running in sand was hard and he soon caught up. "Grab her, Anna!"

Even now, he was considerate enough to keep Anna in their game. She slowed enough so her daughter could reach out and grab on to her shirt with one hand. Fun and fair enough. Then she felt the small fistful of sand get dropped down her back. Dirty rats!

"Anna! You stinker." She squeaked in surprise and laughed as she shimmied the wet sand out of her top.

Daniel slid his sunglasses up to his forehead. She saw the flash of fire in his eyes that went far beyond playing. He let her see it, too, and the small thrill sliced through her center. Maybe he *was* interested?

"You're a cheater, Daniel Delaney." Empty words to cover her reaction. Then he grinned and she knew he'd felt that little zing, too. "I'm hungry. Anyone up for a burger?"

"And a milk shake?" Anna added hopefully.

"Yeah, she needs a milk shake to wash down the ice cream cone we had about an hour ago," Daniel interjected.

"Oh!" Keela giggled. "You little conniver! You'll have to catch me if you want that milk shake now."

And their second chase began, zigzagging all the way back to the sidewalk.

"Ah, geez, we forgot the crutches." Daniel eased Anna onto a bench, then took off at a sprint to fetch the forgotten crutches on the sand.

"Did you have fun, sweetcakes?"

"He's silly. I love him."

At the heartfelt and innocent outburst, all Keela could think to do was take her daughter into her arms and hug her. *Oh, honey, don't get your heart broken again.* Watching Daniel Delaney saunter up the beach with Anna's crutches, she immediately decided she should heed her own warning.

Soon enough, shoes back on, sand dusted off, they set off for the Busy Bee Diner—the old-school eatery overrun with cutesy oversize yellow-and-black-striped bee decorations—for shakes and burgers. The stroll up Main Street past The Drumcliffe Hotel felt suspiciously like a family outing, and it gave Keela pause. Secretly, she had a daring wish it could be so but quickly reeled it back. It was a dangerous thought, one that could end with hurt and sorrow. She had personal proof of that with Ron. But when was the last time her daughter had laughed this much, or felt part of something bigger than just the two of them? That was what Daniel Delaney had brought into their lives, whether he'd wanted to or not.

A memory or two popped into her thoughts. Back in the days when Ron had seemed a different man, and Anna was young enough to enjoy everything, they'd had times like this. Anna might have been too little to remember, though. But Keela would never forget. She'd once come to America seeking her dream, she'd married and had a family…but it had all fallen apart. Now she was just starting to put her life back together as a confident, independent woman, and she wasn't sure she could ever risk putting Anna, or herself, through anything as horrible as the divorce again.

Yet there was Daniel, making sure Anna could keep up with his slow pace, telltale sand on his arms and neck, evidence of their fun adventures by the sea. Anna's unruly hair had come loose from the pigtails, making her look like a wild child. A completely happy wild child. Then there was Daniel with his bun-hugging jeans, soaked T-shirt and messed-up hair, looking sexy as hell.

Hadn't the guy once saved a seal, a *selkie*? What could be sexier than that?

They reached the entrance to the old-time diner, a huge, happy-looking cartoon bee greeting them on the glass door. Daniel's contented-looking eyes found hers and a tiny thrill settled behind her navel. Keela sucked in her stomach.

"Can we sit at the counter?" Anna blurted.

"Sure." Daniel didn't hesitate to answer but took his time changing the focus of his gaze from Keela to Anna. Maybe he'd felt something, too.

The guy did all the right things. Now all she had to do was convince herself to take a chance again.

"Hey, I'm buying, by the way." Keela had tip money burning a hole in her pocket and couldn't think of two more worthy people to spend it on.

Chapter Five

Keela's phone rang on Sunday.

"Keela? It's Maureen. I was so busy with the quilters yesterday I didn't get a chance to tell you what great feedback I got from the hotel guests."

It was noon and Keela had just made a peanut butter and blueberry jam sandwich for Anna, who sat happily at the kitchen table putting baked potato chips between the slathered slices of bread and crunching down.

"That's wonderful." She mindlessly walked to the couch and sat, happy for the news.

"They couldn't say enough nice things about you. Evidently you have a gentle and healing touch."

"Oh, I don't know about that, but thanks for letting me know." It'd been good to put time on hold and perform the rites of relaxation and good health for her clients. She'd forgotten how good.

"I'd like to invite you to dinner tonight as my way of

saying thanks," Daniel's mom was saying. "We close down the pub at five on Sundays so we can all have dinner together away from the restaurant guests. Can you come? We eat around six."

Being invited to the Delaney Sunday dinner felt like an honor she was nowhere near worthy of, yet she'd heard the words and couldn't think of anyplace she'd rather be, especially if Daniel would be there. "I'd love to."

"Of course, Anna is invited, too."

"That's grand. Thanks so much." She'd been so carried away by the invitation, she'd momentarily forgotten about the little one having a quiet chat with herself over lunch in the other room, who'd now gone conspicuously quiet.

"Daniel will come by to pick you up around five thirty."

"Oh, that's not necessary. I can drive over."

"I know, but he wants to come get you."

There was the part that tripped her up. Was Maureen arranging this between them, or was Daniel a willing participant? If so, why wasn't he the one to call?

After having the nicest afternoon and early dinner with Daniel at the Busy Bee yesterday, he'd walked them both back to her car at the hotel parking lot, patted Anna's head goodbye, then looked wistfully into Keela's eyes and said good-night with a mere squeeze of her upper arm. Why would he want to drive over to pick her up when he'd obviously been keeping a safe distance between them?

Keela sensed he held back a lot where she was concerned. The fact she'd be returning to work on Monday and he'd be her boss again probably had a lot to do with his being cautious. Still, there were those moments when her gaze eagerly latched on to his. When all kinds of crazy thoughts flew through her mind and sensations through her body. Positive he'd felt something, too, she only wished she could figure out what kept him from acting on it.

Don't push things. That was her takeaway after the dinner at her house, where she'd obviously made him uncomfortable. Then yesterday, there were times when it felt like they were one happy family—especially horsing around at the beach—and he seemed a completely willing participant. Yet others where she still sensed it was hard for him to interact with Anna.

Then he'd rushed an underwhelming goodbye in the parking lot. An arm squeeze?

Talk about mixed messages!

Now she'd been invited to the family dinner and she hadn't a clue if Daniel had requested it or if he'd been coerced by his overeager mother to bring her. Though she'd clearly said otherwise. Still, confused or not, having dinner at the Delaney pub made Keela smile. She missed big family dinners.

She watched dust motes float in the sunlight through her front window and remembered the tour of the pub Padraig Delaney had taken her on the day of his eighty-fifth birthday. Tucked in the back corner of the hotel restaurant, where huge windows at the front and along all sides ensured gorgeous ocean views from every angle, were double doors. On the glass panels, classic cursive script spelled out *Padraig's* on one side and *Pub* on the other. He'd swung the doors open to a beautiful midcentury modern version of a pub. Heavy with wood, the dated American-style bar was long and clean, with varnished oak floors and rows of round, dark wood tables and leather-topped stools. The actual bar was classic mahogany, but not ornate, and it was the only area that had high-backed stools that rested on top of small seventies-era checkerboard tile. The distinct aroma of beer had sat heavy in the room, and the head of the Delaney clan had been proud to point out the long row of draft beer dispensers, but also how he kept the sacred Guinness faucet separated from all the others.

"Biggest choice of beers in these parts," he'd said, like a king in his castle.

Padraig had also bragged how he'd had the decorative round lights and four lamppost fixtures shipped all the way from County Sligo back home. She'd remembered seeing lights like those not so long ago along the River Fergus and on Parnell Street in Ennis, her hometown. He'd also mentioned how Maureen and Sean had insisted on adding tray ceilings to "class" the place up about twenty years back. Which did make the ceiling feel higher and, combined with the pub's view, bigger.

The main difference from other Irish bars and Padraig's Pub was the fact it wasn't dark or dingy inside. That was thanks to three circular windows spaced out in the long outside wall, showcasing the Pacific Ocean just across the road.

Keela smiled and imagined having dinner with the Delaney family in the far back corner in the pub, where she'd noticed a long and weathered dining table. Sudden nostalgia for her family took hold and her eyes moistened. She'd left so much behind, but if she hadn't ventured to California, she never would have had her beautiful daughter.

"Who was that?" Anna came shuffling into the room and, after resting the crutches against the arm, plopped beside her on the couch.

"Mrs. Delaney just invited us for dinner. What do you think about that?"

"That's supertastic!"

Content like she hadn't been in ages, Keela was inclined to agree.

Ten feet from the pub door, Daniel slowed and tugged Keela's hand. She stopped and turned. "No matter what happens tonight," he said, "or whatever is said or implied by my family, you and I are what we decide to be."

She gave him an odd look. "Should I be worried?"

"Not at all. Well, maybe a little. It's my family and they can be overbearing. Grandda likes to say outrageous things. Don't hold that against me."

She gave a nervous laugh, maybe not completely understanding. "Is my job secure?"

"Always will be." Then he took a breath and swung open the pub door.

He had to work extra hard to avoid his grinning grandfather's stare when he entered with Keela and Anna in tow. Still, Patrick made a point of tugging him aside. "She's a woman a man could warm to," he whispered with a wink.

So subtle, Gramps.

Also his mother's quiet yet pleased expression seemed downright suspicious. Were they in cahoots, playing matchmaker? If they were, Daniel would put a stop to it later. It had been his idea to invite and pick up the dinner guests, and he'd let his mother make the call only because she wanted the invitation to be part of her thank-you to Keela. They were his friends first, and if he wanted to invite them, he would. He didn't need his family's encouragement.

After all the time he'd spent with Keela lately, things

were beginning to feel like dating. Not on his agenda! Especially now, after landing the community college account. Yet here he was, unable to resist sitting next to Keela, but putting Anna between them at the long pub table—it was the right thing to do, since he'd invited them—and being glad they were there. He couldn't very well bring them to supper, then abandon them. He made the mistake of glancing at Grandda again and couldn't look away fast enough before seeing that smug, toothy grin.

Did you know that the name Keela in Irish means "beauty that only poetry can capture"?

He did now, but he'd always sworn he'd been born without the poetry gene, a shameful shortcoming for an Irishman. All Daniel could hope was that Keela didn't feel half the pressure he was getting.

"Potatoes?" Keela handed him the huge bowl of mashed potatoes over Anna's head after first serving her daughter.

He liked how her accent made the word sound like *"bah-day-tus,"* the same way his grandfather said it. No wonder the old guy liked her. This part of the family meal, right after Grandda said a short grace, was always fast and furious as the dishes got passed from both directions.

Conor always planned his dinner break to the T in order not to miss the extra special meal on Sunday nights. If he didn't show, they all knew there had to be some kind of law enforcement emergency. Tonight he handed the gravy across the table to Daniel as if reading his mind. *Got potatoes, need gravy.* But he also made an inquisitive lift of brows in the direction of Keela as he did. *What gives?* those sea-blue, kid-brother eyes seemed to ask.

Daniel braced himself for a grilling later, back at their shared three-bedroom suite. No wonder Grandda was trying to marry them all off, they were taking up hotel rental space!

What gives? That was the big question of the night. Was he or wasn't he dating Keela, and if he was, wasn't it about time he admitted it and considered taking it to the next level? Actually ask her out? He cringed, remembering his chaste squeeze of her arm yesterday evening, when what he'd really wanted to do was kiss her. In front of Anna? Somehow that didn't seem right. Why confuse the kid, when he was confused enough for both of them?

"Someone's bought that B and B across the street." Sean Delaney brought up the safe subject, and Daniel was grateful for the change in topic.

"It's about time," Grandda said.

"We don't need the competition." Maureen chimed in, snatching a dinner roll and passing the basket on. "That's why I'm stepping up the amenities with our guests. Keela did a great job as our part-time masseuse yesterday. Thank you, darlin'."

Keela blushed and bowed her head, humble and so damned appealing.

"Anyone interested in giving nature walks?" his mother added.

"There won't be competition," Mark said. "Places like that appeal to a different crowd than we get here." He spoke for the first time that night, and Daniel noticed he wasn't the only one who was surprised. "And don't look at me for the nature walks." About to slather butter on a roll, he raised the butter knife for dramatic effect. "Surfing lessons, maybe."

Mark's reputation as surfing hero still stood in Sandpiper Beach, even though it was a title he'd earned in his teens, long before he'd enlisted in the army. He had half a dozen trophies to prove it.

"Hey, that's a great idea!" Daniel was happy to hear his brother volunteer for anything after the tough year he'd had. Working full-time as the hotel fix-it guy since getting honorably discharged from the service surely couldn't be satisfying. Though Daniel suspected it was the kind of solitary and serene work a vet with ongoing, though improving, PTSD preferred.

"Oh, I'm going to write that down." Maureen smiled. "Surfing lessons. Wonderful! Any other ideas?"

"How about beer tasting?" Grandda spoke up.

Sean hesitated but responded soon enough. "Da, we don't want to encourage people to get drunk."

"Drunk! From tasting beer? There's no such thing." Padraig feigned insult and shoved in a forkful of food as his eyes sought out Keela. "Ever heard of such a silly notion?" he asked, his mouth full.

She gave her usual melodic laugh, and if Daniel's ears could, they would smile over the lovely sound. He glanced her way, and when their eyes met, hers seemed to be sparkling in the dim pub light. Why did she have to be his employee?

Anna's bedtime dictated an early departure after Maureen's apple spice cake. As Daniel walked the little girl and her mom to their doorstep, Keela lightly touched his forearm—that was another thing he liked about her; she was a toucher when she talked. "Can you stay on for a bit?" she asked.

"Sure." It was time to take that risk—to kiss her. To find out if there was something there or not. "Say goodnight to Daniel, Anna."

The obviously tired little one put her crutches against

the couch and waited for him to kneel down in front of her, then gave him a big hug, complete with hugging noises. *Ooh!* He smiled, even as he tensed. "Sleep tight, bug." The term came out before he'd had a chance to think.

Great, now he was giving nicknames to the squirt.

But Anna beamed at the tag. "I'm not a bug!" she exclaimed, pretending to be insulted.

"What should I call you, then?" If he wanted to date the mom, he needed to get used to the kid, and to be honest, being around her now wasn't half the torture it'd been at first.

She thought intently for a second or two. "Sweetie?"

"That's what I call you." Keela faked concern.

"How about Anna-bug?" Daniel suggested.

With her arms akimbo, Anna acted like he'd just said the dumbest thing in the world. "I guess so." That surprised him. So now she had a nickname, and he still wasn't sure it was a good idea for a kid who already had a dad. Especially with the way his feelings had been building for Keela.

"All right, Anna-bug it is." He high-fived her. When Keela got in on the action, first slapping hands with her daughter, then him, something came over him. His fingers interlaced and tightened around hers, holding her hand in the air a second longer than he should to make his point. After a short pause, she curved her fingers over his. Then he made sure she was looking straight at him when he slowly smiled.

Her huge, appreciative blue eyes told a story he was more than ready to hear…but only after Anna got put to bed. So he let go of Keela's hand and sat on the couch, happy to wait.

Sharing a kiss with a woman wasn't the same as

loving someone who didn't love him back. If he kissed Keela, it would just be a kiss with a lady he was extremely attracted to, not desperately in love with. Why not give it a try? What could it hurt?

That was the problem: hurt was his old friend. He'd been dragging it around with him ever since Emma had died and Kathryn had left. Wasn't it time to move on from Kathryn, though never forgetting Emma? Keela, being an employee, wasn't exactly the ideal person to move on with, though he understood there would never be a perfect situation. Still. They worked together!

Finally, Keela came quietly into the room, ending his ongoing inner battle. Her expression seemed shy, this from a person who never had a problem stating her mind. He liked that he might have some effect on her like that.

He patted the cushion next to him and she obliged. When she sat, a whiff of a light tropical flower scent invigorated his thoughts. "So, I get the feeling something's going on between us, am I right?" Why not be straightforward?

Her smile was demure, again unlike her. "Correct."

"The question is, what are we supposed to do about it?" He took her hand in his and laced fingers again.

"Is there a problem?"

"I think so."

"Because I work for you?"

"Part of the problem, yes." He took a moment to formulate his words. "You've spoken about your divorce some at work, and I've seen firsthand how disappointed you've been with men. American men."

"Just Ron." She sighed.

"Now see, that's another concern. He's a bad example for men. That makes two reasons not to…" How should he put it?

"Not to what? Explore this little gift that's dropped in our laps?"

A gift? She thought of getting involved with him as a gift? The idea helped put the dilemma in perspective. "So you're attracted to me, too?"

A light puff of air escaped her lips—a frustrated laugh because he was being dense? "I've obviously done a terrible job of letting you know." Her cheeks flushed pink.

He needed to warn her. "I had a bad experience with a woman not too long ago. I'll be honest and say it's made me gun-shy. So I'm just saying I've loved and been hurt, and so have you. So that's three reasons I'm fighting my instincts right now."

Empathy filled her eyes. "I've wondered about that, your being hurt before, and you know I understand, right?"

Her concern touched him. "I guess if anyone could, it would be you." And that helped make up his mind. He was through resisting her, for tonight, anyway.

Keela had the same desire as Daniel. She wanted more than anything to kiss him. Just now he'd explained why he'd been so hesitant. *If anyone could understand, she did.* Then she saw the shift in his demeanor. The questioning employer stepped out and in his place was a man who'd made up his mind. A very appealing man who knew how to treat a lady respectfully, how to fix faucets and run a business. One whose thick dark hair called out to have fingers run through it. His forest-green eyes searched hers and she sent the strongest message she could telepathically—*I really want to kiss you.*

Now that she'd made up her mind, he didn't act fast enough for her liking, so she leaned forward, put her hand on his smoothly shaved cheek and pulled him closer. She wanted to kiss him for a hundred different reasons, but mostly because he was a great guy, and she'd missed being in a man's arms. Of all the men she'd known over the years, he seemed the most trustworthy.

But it wasn't his safeness that appealed to her, it was the tingles he created across her neck whenever he looked at her like this, and how she always tightened her core whenever he got close. Not because he made her nervous, but because without trying he always caused a reaction in her. This was the guy she wanted to find out about, even though it scared her, and now her mouth was closer to his than it'd ever been before. Keela eased her eyes shut, savoring his delicious woodsy scent as she moved closer.

"This still isn't a good idea," he whispered just above her mouth, close enough for her to sense the pulse in his neck.

"Who says?" she breathed, savoring how his words had tickled her lips. Then she closed the tiny gap and kissed him.

In an instant he took over their kiss, letting her know exactly how interested he was and who was in charge. She liked it, too. Soon she relaxed into the delectable sensation of locking lips with Daniel Delaney. She opened her mouth, indulging in touching the tip of his tongue with hers, tasting mint he must have popped while she put Anna to bed, and basking in the waterfall of sensations trickling from the top of her head to the tips of her breasts. It'd been years since she'd enjoyed a kiss this much.

Daniel stopped short of caressing her breast, though

he wanted to more than anything. He'd admitted to himself that he'd thought about touching her plenty of times at work. Talk about an HR nightmare. He wanted to do a lot more to her than that, too. Some boss he was. Yet now, when he had the chance, he drew the line, and cupping her was on the wrong side. *Not tonight. Take it slow. You've got to look her in the eyes tomorrow at work, and that needs to be all business.*

To avoid the soft and inviting real estate sitting right beneath his fingers, his for the taking, he went off on a tangent of kissing the side of her neck and nibbling her earlobe, and he struck gold. He'd found one of her special spots, judging from how she moaned and arched her back. It would be so easy to take a breast into his palm…and who knew where that would lead.

Nope. This was what he'd been worried about—not wanting to stop once he'd started kissing and touching Keela. He found his way back to her mouth, and she'd obviously been revved up, given the vigorous greeting he received. The lady knew how to kiss, and all kinds of nerve endings were coming to life because of it.

Making out felt great, and he'd missed it. A lot. Oh, but he'd already drawn the line, so when his hand almost settled on her chest again, he quickly moved to her upper arms and squeezed.

Then he broke off the kiss. "Wow."

Those wide pupils in her dreamy eyes communicated that he could have gone a lot further. Another thing he'd been worried about: she was on board. Totally. He'd really liked kissing her, wanted more; what fool wouldn't. But he still wasn't ready for everything else his body wanted, and the baggage it would drag along. On both sides.

Getting to know Keela would have to be a one-step-at-a-time dance. Tonight he'd kissed her. Finally. And there was definitely something there.

He cupped her cheek with his palm and stared into those mesmerizing blue eyes for a few long moments, wanting nothing more than to kiss those lips again. Instead he pecked the tip of her nose and pulled back.

Abrupt? Maybe, but it was what he needed to do. This was the first step and he'd have to decide when and where to take the next. No, it wasn't fair that she couldn't have a say in it, especially since she was so enthusiastic, but he needed to feel in control. Kathryn had been the one in control before, and it had nearly broken him, so ending their kiss just now was his way of taking the lead. It was safer that way, because being honest, he could've stuck around and kissed Keela for hours.

Keela was confused. She'd let down her guard and gone passionate with Daniel. Then he'd ended it. Had she done something wrong? The little voice in the back of her head tried to mention he was her boss, but she'd shut it down. Immediately. And she was glad she had, because her suspicions about having some great chemistry with the man had been true. Wow. Still, knowing that frightened her.

She'd thought she had good chemistry with Ron, too. Got pregnant pretty darn fast as a result, and that was when everything had changed. He'd looked at her differently, treated her with less care, become a nitpicker, sending the clear message that she never quite measured up.

She hadn't tried to trap him, but she'd always suspected that was how he'd felt. Ron had done the honorable thing, married her, probably because he'd brought her all the way to the United States to seduce her. Well, maybe he should have made sure a condom had been adequate enough. She'd been so naive then, she wasn't even on birth control.

Things were different now, and she needed to remind herself of that. She was a grown woman who was attracted to Daniel, and he was obviously attracted to her. But she still wasn't on birth control! Mainly because after the divorce, she'd sworn off men. Who needed sex? Not that one make-out session necessarily meant they'd jump into bed with each other anytime soon. Especially since they worked together.

Still, note to self: see gynecologist for prescription... just in case.

Wishful thinking? Probably.

"It'll be an early day for you tomorrow," Daniel said, gazing into her eyes, "so I don't want to keep you up too late."

She needed time to refocus after his mind-blowing kisses and her overthinking everything. "Oh, right. You've got a point."

He stood and reached for her hand. She took it and followed him from the couch to the door. There, after one short and chaste kiss, he hugged her tight. It felt wonderful to be held again. She wanted nothing more than to rest her head on his muscular chest for the rest of the night. But why rush things? Especially since there was still that pesky little issue of birth control pills. Maybe it was a good thing he'd so abruptly ended their make-out session, because apparently, from the way he made her feel, she was a girl who couldn't say no to Daniel Delaney.

"Good night," he said.

"Good night." She tried her best not to sound too

dreamy. "I'll see you tomorrow." She watched him walk down the steps to his car with mixed feelings.

Truth was, they were both adults. He'd told her tonight he'd had a bad breakup. Well, welcome to the club. They could be good for each other in that regard, both venturing back into a relationship after being devastated by love. Scary stuff, that. But there was still another major issue with having a relationship with Daniel. He was her boss, and that couldn't change because she needed her job.

After Daniel had kissed Keela again on the doorstep and said good-night under the guise of making sure she got enough rest before going back to work tomorrow, he drove home with multiple thoughts competing for attention. He needed to face the fact that he was involved with an employee. Never a good idea. Another thing he needed to consider was her daughter—still a tender subject for him. Things could get very confusing for little Anna, too, if their dating didn't work out.

Yet those crazy thoughts planted in his head by his grandfather kept popping up. Could she be the one the old man insisted she was? Would he be a fool to pass this up? If so, was he ready to be a father figure, too? A chance he'd lost with Emma, and hadn't thought he'd ever get again. Yet that was the deal with Keela *and* Anna.

He drove, hardly noticing where he was, depending on rote memory to take him to the hotel. Where should he go from here? He'd kissed her and really liked it, and definitely wanted more.

He slammed on the brakes, almost running a red light, then chided himself for moving too fast. Ha, Keela might not agree with him on that, but what they'd done tonight felt damn fast from where he sat. She didn't have a clue what he'd been through, how low he'd sunk before pulling himself back together and moving on after Kathryn and baby Emma.

Plus, now he had the community college work to think about. Their summer football program would ensure he'd be super busy treating the team's various aches and injuries. He'd barely have time for himself, let alone dating again. And Anna. He couldn't leave her out of the equation.

He was a doctor and a businessman whose practice came first. Was there room for more?

As he pulled into his parking spot at the hotel, he thought about little Anna and the painful twinges he still felt around her, and how her gorgeous mother both excited and scared him. Would Keela understand that life needed to be all work and no play for a while longer? Or would she soon figure out what an emotional mess he was, and how he kept avoiding her, and give up?

He didn't want her to.

Chapter Six

Monday morning the clinic got off to a roaring start. Every appointment for the day had been booked, and thanks to a Sunday afternoon ankle injury sustained by playing Frisbee with his dog, one of the star athletes from the 4Cs football team got double booked with Daniel's first appointment.

Keela showed up early. "Good morning, Dr. Delaney," she said, a certain sparkle in her eyes.

"Welcome back, Keela." He let a hint of his thoughts loose with the greeting, appreciating how terrific she looked back in uniform. They shared a quick but knowing gaze that warmed up his blood. Man, he'd missed her at work. He'd missed her just since last night, too.

To hell with all work and no play. Since only the two of them were there, he followed his gut and waltzed her into his office, closed the door and kissed her. From her easy participation, he knew she was on board. "So, we should probably talk about this."

"My kissing the boss good-morning?"

"I'm pretty sure the boss just kissed the employee. But look, I never want you to feel pressure from me."

"I like kissing you." She gazed into his eyes, her arms loosely wrapped around his neck.

"Good. But I want you to know that whatever this is—" removing a hand from her waist, he gestured from his chest to her chin "—well, I never want you to feel pressured about anything."

"I promise to speak up, as long as you promise not to let anything happening between us affect my job."

He raised his right hand, hoping she didn't think of him as a slimy, taking-advantage kind of boss. "You have my word."

"Good. Now shut up and kiss me again."

The second kiss felt intimate and brought him to his senses. Things could get serious with Keela quickly. Midkiss, they heard the back entry door slam closed, and stopped.

She used her thumb to wipe a trace of her lipstick off his mouth, then winked. He swung the office door open and they stepped into the hallway, hoping their compromising situation didn't look too obvious. This business was his livelihood, as well as Keela's. It was a big responsibility, and his reputation could be at stake.

He quickly shifted to all-business mode. "Morning, Phil," he called down the hall, ignoring the hint of disappointment in Keela's gaze.

"Hey, boss." His temporary employee stepped out of the locker area.

"This is Keela, and, Keela, this is Phil." He liked how that singular blue-eyed glance from Keela had the same effect as a quick cup of coffee on his pulse, though that probably had more to do with kissing her. Whatever, he was happy to have her back on the job. But he didn't like how Phil was anything but discreet in checking her out, so he grabbed the appointment printout from the in-tray and handed it to the temporary PT to distract him. "I'm having you two work together today, since we've got several group appointments scheduled in the treatment room. That work for you guys?"

Phil looked happier than he should about the arrangement. That bugged the hell out of Daniel, and he wondered if he could make a quick executive decision and separate them, but he didn't have a chance. His 8:00 a.m. add-on had just shown up, noticeably limping.

Keela grabbed the list from Phil and they soon set off, playing tag-team with their lineup of treatments. Daniel enjoyed hearing her boss the temp around, not the least bit interested in making small talk with the guy. Good.

Over the course of the morning, running in and out of examination rooms, Daniel also overheard some outbursts from Keela. "Where're the stretch bands? Are we out of heel protectors?"

She'd come back in the nick of time to order supplies that had run dangerously low during her absence. Phil might find her enchanting, but from the frustrated and downright impatient looks Keela shot him, Daniel had nothing to worry about.

That was how the week played out. Every single day he hit the office running. Their Monday morning wake-up kiss never got repeated, and with Daniel attending the summer afternoon football practices at the 4Cs, he never once got to tell Keela goodbye or kiss her good-night.

He didn't call her, either.

Coward.

He really was busy, but that busy? It wasn't that he didn't want to call her, but *Work has to come first* became his daily mantra. Or excuse, whichever way he looked at it. Though he definitely missed kissing her.

Being so busy, it seemed like only a blink of an eye before Friday rolled around, and Daniel needed to settle up with Phil and thank him for filling in during Keela's absence.

"I wouldn't have made it through without you, and I'll be happy to write a referral if you're ever looking for full-time work somewhere."

Keela tossed Daniel a warning glance. Later, in private, she approached him.

"How can you give Phil a recommendation?"

"Look, the guy's work skills may not be up to par, but he helped the clinic get by. I owe him something. If another clinic calls regarding the referral, I can give a verbal caveat at that time." Daniel had been running ragged for the last month. "I didn't have the time to give the temp a proper orientation or evaluation."

"Which is why you should have let me come back earlier."

He used his charming face. "Well, you're back now." It got the reaction he'd hoped for.

She looked left and right, and since no one was within view, she popped a quick kiss on his lips, and zap, there was that feeling again.

Why the hell hadn't he brought her back sooner?

Knowing Keela would be around from here on out brought peace of mind that the clinic would run smoothly again. The only problem was it would be extremely difficult to keep her out of his mind and to focus solely on the job.

Did he really want to avoid her, or was that just the way things needed to be for now? He'd take the nonstop pace of the clinic as a gift of time to figure things out. That was, if he ever got a chance to think.

Phil had left, and so had Abby, the receptionist, for the day, so it was just the two of them. Of course, Daniel had to run to the 4Cs for the evening football scrimmage, but right now Keela gazed expectantly at him.

"Nice to have you back," he said, thinking how lame it sounded.

"It's great to be back."

"Grab a quick bite with me?" Even a simple request like that sent doubt threading through his veins.

"I'm going to stay late, if you don't mind, and get all the supply orders up to date," she said. "What a mess."

"Oh, great. Thanks." Was the sudden feeling relief or disappointment? "What about Anna?"

"Mrs. Jenkins offered to keep her. They're going to order pizza and watch a movie."

He nodded. "Sorry I haven't been around for you much this week."

She shook her head, her beautifully shaped brows nearly coming together. "It's been manic all week. You've been running like a madman. I understand."

He wanted to ask her if she was doing anything tomorrow afternoon, but he couldn't guarantee he'd be done with the morning football practice to keep his word, so rather than risk coming off like her ex and canceling last minute, he let the opportunity slip by. But something came over him and he opened his arms. "I meant what I said about having you back."

She stepped into his embrace and they stood quietly

hugging, enjoying the moment, unwinding from the busy day together, gently rocking back and forth. And feeling so right. She fit perfectly in his arms, and after working all day, she still smelled great, too. He closed his eyes and inhaled her scent, letting it work its magic on him, savoring their closeness, feeling the extra heat at every point their bodies touched, wishing for time to stand still. She renewed his energy, just by letting him hold her. This would be their little secret, since Monday's stolen kiss, and her surprise peck a few moments ago, and it was the best thirty seconds of the week.

She lifted her chin, gazing serenely at him. It was so easy to get lost in those gorgeous wide eyes, but this time they sent an insistent and obvious message. So he dipped his head and kissed her again. Wow. And just when he was halfway to kissing paradise, the alarm on his cell phone went off, reminding him he had fifteen minutes to make it to the 4Cs practice.

Her coy smile communicated that she understood. For that, he was grateful, yet he knew they were far from finished with moments like these. The thought both excited and made him uneasy. He could get too used to it, and she could change her mind.

"I'll call you tomorrow," he said, dashing for the door.

By noon on Saturday, Keela had given up on Ron. She was damned if she'd call to remind him today was his daughter's fifth birthday. And it was the second year he'd forgotten, or simply didn't give a bloody care anymore.

It was nearly impossible to paint on a cheery face for Anna; Keela's insides were twisted with anger, and sadness weighed heavy on her heart, yet she did her best to smile. For Anna's sake. Though her eyes stung and she feared she'd break into tears looking into her daughter's huge, expectant stare. How could the man be so heartless?

She should have trusted her instinct and planned a small birthday party for Anna instead of giving Ron a chance to be a hero for a day.

He was so *not* a hero. She knew this for sure, since she'd recently met the real thing. Daniel. Now she'd have to scramble to bake a cake. Thank the heavens she'd bought Anna a special "big girl" backpack for school and had filled it with small presents. At least it was something.

Even Daniel had been missing in action since their hot make-out session last weekend. Sure, they'd stolen a couple of kisses, but they'd been too busy at work to steal any more time together. He hadn't called once all week, either, but when rushing off last night, he'd said he'd phone her today. She glanced at her watch again. Well?

She really couldn't depend on men.

Though one kind thought wouldn't let her get away with writing off Daniel. He'd held her yesterday evening, and being in his arms had felt so inviting. So right. Like she belonged there. Then he'd left without making any plans with her. She understood he was a busy man. In some ways a broken man. Even more reason not to get her hopes up about the guy. Why set herself up for more heartache?

Her phone rang, and she nearly jumped, surprised that her first hope was it might be Daniel, and only a distant second, Ron.

"Keela? It's Maureen. I'm so sorry to call last minute, but I've got a VIP guest requesting a massage out of the blue. Any chance you can come to the hotel this afternoon? I'd be able to watch Anna for you this time."

"Oh, normally I'd love to, but it's Anna's birthday today, so I really can't."

"Oh, how lovely. I totally understand, and I suppose you've got big plans."

"Not really. We're just going to stick around home and have a low-key mommy-daughter day." She'd promised to give Anna a mani-pedi, then watch *Frozen* for the umpteenth time. One of the presents in her backpack was a pretty blue costume like Elsa's dress. Yes, she was getting sick of the movie soundtrack, but it was Anna's favorite. And it was her birthday.

"Well, any chance you could do the massage tomorrow? That might work."

"Sure." Why not? They didn't have any plans.

Daniel was driving home, fighting the weekend beach traffic, when his phone went off. It synced with his car, so he answered, hands free. "Hi, Mom."

"Did you know today's Anna's birthday?"

Keela hadn't said a peep about it all week. Then again, they'd hardly had a chance to talk. "I did not. Are they having a party?"

"I just got off the phone with Keela. Had a client lined up, but she said they were hanging out, having a low-key day. Didn't say anything about a party, just that it was Anna's birthday."

If he'd called her like he should've, he would have known this. "Thanks for the heads-up. She's probably gonna see her dad tomorrow."

"Actually, Keela's coming here for that client massage and I'll be watching Anna tomorrow."

Well, that's not right. A kid deserves a party.

Suddenly he felt confused. Should he do something? He'd been using the busy clinic as a great excuse to steer clear of Keela in an attempt to avoid his feelings about her. But Anna's birthday came only once a year. And, when he let himself admit it, he liked the little squirt. Maybe the immunity was kicking in?

He recklessly cut around the slow car in front of him on the freeway to make his exit and headed for the clinic. He needed to catch up on some paperwork, and he'd agreed to see the kid with the ankle injury again as a follow-up.

After rushing through the appointment and locking up the clinic, he headed straight to the local toy store.

"What would a five-year-old girl like?" he asked the nearest clerk. She walked him and his shopping cart to an aisle lined with bright colors and glitter. Loads of glitter, on everything. Dolls. Costumes. Games. Miniature-sized kitchens. Dollhouses. He'd never felt more out of place in his life.

It hit him midaisle how Emma never got a birthday. He never knew what would set him off, and this time it was a toy store. Old pain beat through him like a sledgehammer, nearly taking his breath away. He went still, grasping the cart for support, trying to get a grip on his emotions, fighting off the profound sadness as it swept through him. It never got easier when it hit. So much for immunity. But today was another little girl's birthday. He had to think about the present, not the past. So he forced himself to continue shopping and eventually the ache behind his sternum let up.

Soon he spotted the perfect gift. And he didn't stop there, tossing item after item into his shopping cart. Thinking only about now, not the past, he found that going overboard for a kid was fun. The even bigger news was he'd managed to ward off the pain and still function. Progress.

"Can you wrap everything for me?"

The clerk's eyes went big. "We'll need some time."

"That's fine. I've got another errand to run. I'll be back in forty minutes." He handed the clerk a twenty to make sure they got right on task with the wrapping, then left.

On a mission, he sped to The Drumcliffe and, taking the back employee entrance, headed for the kitchen. Finding a double chocolate layer cake in the dessert display—one of the pastry chef's specialties—he grabbed it and took it to Rita, the soon-to-retire restaurant chef. "Can you add a name to this and decorate it for a young girl? She likes flowers and her favorite color is yellow." He was surprised he knew that. "Oh, and her name is Anna."

Fifteen minutes later, with a beautiful little-kid-styled cake in hand, he stopped at the freezer, grabbing a carton of mint-chip ice cream. That was the flavor Anna ordered whenever he'd taken her for cones. Out the door he flew, intending to pick up the presents and make it to Keela's before the rock-hard ice cream had a chance to melt.

Once parked at Keela's curb, it took some doing, but he stuck a party blowout in his mouth, picked up the huge toy store bag filled with wrapped gifts in one hand, the cake and ice cream in the other, then juggled his way up the porch steps and knocked with his foot.

Anna didn't beat her mother to the door like she usually did. Instead, Keela opened it. Her hair was pulled back in a low ponytail, her eyes striking as always. Wearing old jeans and a tight blue tank top with black bra straps showing, Keela looked great. More than great. Daniel blew on the party favor.

Keela took one look at him with his arms full of presents, treats and goodies, and burst into tears.

Anna appeared behind her mother in a yellow summery dress, her mouth agape, eyes wide. He had to keep up the glee so the kid wouldn't notice her mother crying. "Are those for me?"

"Who else would they be for, squirt?" he said around the blowout, since his hands were full.

"Wow, Dr. Daniel is just like Kristoff!" she said as she launched herself at his leg.

Keela thought fast, though everything was blurry from happy tears, and grabbed the box with what she assumed held a cake, and the carton of ice cream, not giving Anna a chance to upend anything.

Daniel looked surprised by her tears, but he couldn't possibly know what she'd been going through all morning. The anger, frustration and heartbreak over the fact Ron had missed Anna's birthday, making it two years in a row. Proving he'd become a father on paper only. But she'd promised she wouldn't go there. Not today. Not on Anna's special day. Then she saw Daniel, her boss—her potential boyfriend—doing an extraordinarily sweet thing for her daughter, and lost it. Next week, when she was alone, she'd call and tell Ron to take a hike. Just leave them alone. But today, for the sake of her daughter, she'd painted on a smile and kept it there until she answered the door.

Even with the silly party blowout in his mouth, Daniel beamed right along with Anna as she hugged his leg and hip. How could a lady not fall for a man like that?

"Who's Kristoff?" His muffled question.

"The hero in her favorite animated movie." *The good guy. Whereas Ron had earned the title of Hans, the bad guy hidden beneath a charming grin.*

"He likes ice," Anna chimed in, apparently squeezing Daniel within an inch of his life. "And he has a reindeer."

"Speaking of ice, are you going to let me in or are we gonna let the ice cream melt?"

Anna let go of her death grip and picked up her crutches, heading for the living room couch. "Can I see what's in the bag?"

Keela walked the cake and ice cream to the kitchen, leaving the Santa Claus–sized bag of gifts up to Daniel.

After she put the ice cream in the freezer, she took a peek at the gorgeous cake, so much prettier than hers. She pushed the one she'd hurriedly baked aside to make way for the professional one. Then she returned to the living room and joined Daniel and Anna on the couch. Daniel pulled out party hats and more blowouts and insisted everyone put them on. He also insisted they take a group selfie. "Smile!" Anna giggled her way through several pictures.

"Aren't we supposed to wait until after cake and ice cream to open the presents?" He tried to bargain with Anna.

"No!" she yelled, eyeing the contents of the bag. "I see a Hula-Hoop in there!"

"Well, I guess you can have that one now, since I couldn't wrap it." Daniel pulled the neon-pink hoop out and handed it over. "Just because you can't run doesn't mean you can't stay active, right?"

"Right!" She moved to the middle of the room and, even with her leg in a nearly matching cast, managed to keep the glittery hoop going for several seconds. "See? Just like your grandda taught me at his party."

"Good going." As Daniel watched, he set gift after gift, wrapped in pink, purple and blue strips, on the coffee table. Anna's eyes grew bigger with each one.

"Well, I guess I better get some plates for the cake and ice cream, then," Keela said. "So Anna can open her presents."

"I've got just the thing." Daniel dug deep into the bag, coming up with paper plates that matched their party hats and handing them to Keela.

"You shouldn't have," she said quietly, so that Anna, in her Hula-Hoop frenzy, couldn't hear. Keela's heart was nearly bursting with warmth.

He subtly lifted a brow. "Something tells me I most definitely should have."

Not only was the guy sweet and sensitive, he also turned out to be intuitive.

In shame, she bent her head, or maybe it was anger welling up again for Ron. But she couldn't look at Daniel right then, so she went off to the kitchen.

She moved her small, homemade version of a birthday cake from the table to the counter to make room for the perfect one Daniel had brought. She was hoping to distract herself enough to prevent another bout of crying, when she saw a shadow behind her.

"May I ask why you didn't plan a party?"

Keela cast a quick glance over her shoulder, pretending she was too busy to turn around. "I was foolish enough to leave the day open for her father to step in." She bit her lower lip, forcing down the sadness. "When will I learn?"

"That is cold." Daniel's warm hand gripped her shoulder, bringing comfort.

In the living room she heard Anna counting the number of presents Daniel had brought. *Why couldn't Ron be a doting dad like that? Truth was, he did dote, but on Diesel, not Anna.* "He just doesn't seem to give a damn about her since we moved here. I'll never understand."

"It doesn't make sense, that's for sure." Daniel turned her to face him. "But let's give that girl a party she won't forget, okay?"

Keela fortified herself and gave him a wink. "You're on." She turned back, handing him the fancy cake, now dotted with the five candles she'd planned to put on her hokey homemade cake.

He took it and set it back on the counter. Instead he picked up her cake and transferred the candles to hers, then carried it to the kitchen table. *Yeah, the guy was definitely a Kristoff.* "Don't forget the ice cream," he said.

Filled with a flood of good feelings, she gave a weepy smile before heading to the freezer, adoring how silly and great the man looked wearing a kid-sized party hat. Another thing to like about him: he was sure enough of himself not to worry about appearances. He was honest and sincere and… Well, feeling the way she did at the moment, the list could go on and on. "I noticed you brought her favorite flavor." And observant!

"She'd never forgive me if I brought the wrong kind."

Humble, too.

An hour later, full of cake—since they'd decided to sample pieces of both—and ice cream, Anna played with her assortment of gifts. A build-it-yourself castle, plus building-brick sets for both an adventure camp and a tree house, which would keep her busy for days, putting them together. An adorable, nearly life-size stuffed bulldog she'd instantly named Tuffy was stationed by her side.

"Why didn't *you* plan a birthday party for her?" Daniel asked quietly again.

Keela sighed, trying to figure out how much to tell him. "I thought for sure her father would have plans, since he'd promised last year he'd never miss her birthday again," she whispered. "But honestly, with her leg, I wasn't sure she'd enjoy a party with other little kids because she wouldn't be able to do much."

"That's understandable." He glanced across the small room at Anna concentrating as she put the pink-and-purple castle together. "You need any help?"

"No."

"She's quite good with things like that. I'm amazed you picked the perfect presents."

"Just a hunch. Anyway, I get what you mean about not being able to participate. But kids like parties."

"And you gave her a perfect party." When Keela smiled, she hoped he understood one-tenth of how much his coming today had meant to both of them. He'd literally saved the day! Again.

Anna had gotten money from her Irish and American grandparents from out of state, unaware of their son's neglect toward their granddaughter. Keela and Anna had talked about how hard it would be to buy clothes for school with her cast on, so they'd agreed to wait. In the meantime, she'd let Anna pick out a couple small but special gifts, one from each set of grandparents. "Next year I won't wait for her father. I am so done with that man."

Daniel's expression was hard to interpret, but when he nodded, she took it to mean he liked her decision.

Anna had set up the kids' zoo animal version of

Monopoly while they chatted. "Will you play with me?" How could they refuse?

Anna seemed to have the run of the board during the second game, thanks to some obvious mistakes by Daniel.

"When can I use my sand baking kit?"

"The next time you go to the beach," Daniel said, taking his turn with the dice and moving his small dog on the game board.

"Will you take me?"

"Sure, but it might be a while, since I'm really busy with work."

"What about right now?"

Keela laughed as Daniel got railroaded by her daughter. Good guy that he was, he suggested they all take a late-afternoon drive to the beach.

She'd had a great opinion of the man since the day he'd hired her, but today he'd become nothing short of a true hero. Who deserved a reward. "I wasn't planning anything fancy for dinner, but can you stay for hamburgers later?" Keela asked on their way out the door.

He pulled her close in a sideways hug. "Sure. I'll even grill them if you have a barbecue."

She wrapped her arm around his waist and smiled as they all walked to her car, since it had Anna's booster seat. Somehow, a day that had gotten off to a horrible start had managed to right itself in a wonderful way. Thanks to her boss.

Hours later Keela put Anna to bed. She'd insisted many birthday gifts from both her mom and Daniel got put on her bed, leaving her and her cast-wrapped leg hardly any room to move. He'd been completely aware how the entire afternoon and evening had felt like a family affair, with him stepping in as the surrogate father, and it gave him pause. Was he ready to take over that kind of role? Wouldn't it be easier to date a woman without that extra component?

But that woman wouldn't be Keela.

He leaned back on the couch, hands behind his head, wondering if he was making the right move, getting more and more involved with the two of them. But not for long, because he glanced up in time to see Keela rush through the doorway and launch herself at him.

On reflex, he opened his arms for her and she dived into them, soon planting a kiss that made his toes curl. Today he didn't resist anything she had in mind, and along with gratefully getting involved in her eager make-out session, he let his hands do some exploring. Every inch of her back felt great, but he wanted more. Those black bra straps had been calling out to him all afternoon, so he ran his fingers underneath them, tugging outward, helping them drop off her shoulders, and fortunately, the tank top straps followed, for an extra sexy look. Though she didn't need any help in that department, not with her straddling his hips and using her tongue in new and inventive ways around his ears and neck. He kissed her throat, enjoying the sweet taste of her skin and the telltale scent of her morning shower. God, she felt great sitting on top of him, squirming with desire.

He found her bottom and pulled her close to the heat stirring inside his jeans, kissing her deeper and soon discovering she wanted him as much as he wanted her. She unzipped him and her hand slipped inside, and through the cotton of his briefs her fingers traced the length of him. He sucked in a breath as his own fingers skimmed the soft flesh bulging over the lacy black bra cups, and he nuzzled, then kissed between her breasts.

When he did, she clutched his erection tighter and he nearly saw stars.

"What do you say we take these off?" she said, tugging at his jeans.

"I want to get *that* off." He reached for the clasp on her bra and she let him.

Looking sexier than ever, with her hair messed up, her skin pink and warm, she stopped, casting a thoughtful glance over her shoulder. "Maybe we should go in there?"

He'd had a straight-line view into her bedroom all afternoon, thanks to her leaving the door open—and more than once that exact same thought had crossed his mind. "Maybe we should."

A half hour later, naked, sweaty and completely satisfied, Daniel lay spread-eagle on Keela's sheets, her soft, warm body crumpled on top of him. She'd nearly driven him nuts. In a good way. A completely amazing and mind-blowing kind of way. One hand traced the curve of her back and hips, until he found her smooth bottom and held on. Give him a few minutes and he'd be good to go again.

"You've restored my faith in men," she mumbled against his chest, just before lifting her head and smiling at him.

"I was that good, huh?"

She laughed and cuffed him. "That, too, but I'm talking about your showing up here and literally saving the day."

"Is that what turned you on so much? Man, I'll have to do that more often."

She cuffed him playfully again and he slipped out of her as she rolled to cuddle beside him. Skin to skin, he held her near and decided he hadn't felt this great or alive in ages. Everything about Keela turned him on, especially her eagerness to make love with him. He rolled toward her, his leg lying over her hip. He played with her hair, remembering the oh-so-sexy sounds she'd made when he'd brought her all the way there. Man, he was getting turned on again just thinking about it. Of course, having her naked and beside him probably had a lot to do with that growing feeling.

But he couldn't dance away from what she'd just said about him restoring her faith in men, and the responsibility it dropped in his currently sexually satiated lap. Near panic set in. Was he ready for this? Getting involved with Keela and taking on the role of—of what, a father for Anna?

He tried not to let on what he was going through, but Keela must have picked up on how he'd inadvertently tensed.

She lifted her head. "You okay?"

Building panic licked at him. He fought it off but couldn't. Was getting close to another woman a setup for more pain? "I just remembered I've got to get up early to be at the Sunday morning practice." He disengaged from her beautiful body, fighting two minds, one that wanted more than anything to spend the night, and the other, the one currently driving the show, wanting to protect him and get the hell out of there. He tried to compromise. "I'd really like to stick around, but I'm afraid I've got to go." *Afraid* being the key word.

She looked disappointed, and maybe hurt? "I understand." So unconvincing.

Disengaging more, he sat up and patted her hip, then lightly kissed her forehead. "This was great, by the way. I never expected anything. I want to make sure you understand that."

"Of course I do. And besides, it was my idea."

He gave a faint smile. "No regrets from me." Lying through his teeth. He'd had no business getting mixed up with a lady who'd only been let down by men, because he was bound to do the same, beginning right now. Could he still blame Kathryn, or was it time to own the fear of getting close?

Whatever the reasons, giving one last pat to her perfectly curved hip, he got off the bed, dressed and left.

Chapter Seven

Keela grabbed her head and rolled around on her bed. What had she done? She didn't do casual sex, didn't even understand what it was. Yet here she was, lying naked in bed, her body still buzzing from Daniel's touch, after watching him leave. He'd been an incredible and attentive lover, but what did that matter if jumping in the sack was all wrong in the first place?

The front door closed. She went back to cringing, suffering the consequences from her self-inflicted wound—jumping his bones on impulse. Her boss, no less!

When would she ever learn she didn't have a clue when it came to picking men? She'd obviously scared him away. By being too forward? He'd been just as enthusiastic as she had, and man, he knew what he was doing, too. And then she'd told him he'd restored her faith in men. Of course she'd scared him away. No clue how to take things slowly. Talk about a turnoff.

She'd been so glad to see him when he'd shown up at her door. He'd done the sweetest, kindest and most amazing thing by bringing a birthday party to Anna. What woman wouldn't fall for a guy like that? In that instant he'd become true hero material. And after a wonderful afternoon and evening, with all kinds of sexy looks zipping between them, she'd lost sight of her judgment to the point of seducing him. What had she been thinking?

Thanks?

No! She didn't do grateful sex any more than she did casual sex. She'd come on to him because she'd wanted to for four months. Because, as well as being sexy in his own way, he was also a responsible and caring adult. She'd seen how he treated his patients at the clinic. He respected people. Through his actions, he'd always made her feel worthy and valued. The guy regularly sent tingles up her arms while she watched him interact with patients. Of course, she'd suppressed the attraction at work and figured she'd never have the nerve to come on to him. Until tonight. After his efforts for her daughter reinforced what an utterly great guy he was.

A guy who'd single-handedly saved her little girl's birthday. Superheroes didn't come any bigger than that.

As she continued to roll around and groan on her bed, she couldn't even blame her actions on alcohol, since the only thing they'd drunk all afternoon had been soda. Yet she'd literally jumped on him and unzipped his pants, feeling wanted by him and freer than at any other time in her life. And he'd obviously liked it, too. Then she'd ruined everything by saying those words. Ugh!

What had she done?

Too much, obviously. Now the ball was in Daniel's

court, and like the fool she was, she'd set herself up to wait for him to take the next step.

"Ahh!" She sat up as she let out her frustration, quickly grabbing a pillow and covering her face, hoping she wouldn't wake Anna. Then she tiptoed to the bathroom with the perfectly working faucets, thanks to the *clever* Daniel Delaney.

What had she done?

Monday morning Daniel was surprised and disappointed to find Keela had called in sick. He'd totally screwed up Saturday, not spending the night. But the thought of staying, and the implications of getting close to a woman again, had sent him running. Plus it would've been so awkward seeing Anna the next morning. What would the squirt think?

He should've called on Sunday. Bad form. But he wasn't sure what to say. Now he'd obviously hurt Keela's feelings, and she was avoiding him.

Another reason to never get involved with an employee!

He sucked in the doubt, picked up the phone and dialed her number. "You okay?"

She sounded subdued when she answered, "Got a horrible headache. Sorry to leave you in the lurch."

She wouldn't lie—he knew her work ethic. "I had Abby call Phil back for today."

"Good. Thanks," she said, after a long pause. "I'm allowed sick days working for you."

"Of course. Hey, we talked about this already. Whatever we do outside of work won't affect anything here. Please understand that." *I'm not a sleazy scoundrel.*

"Thank you. I need my job."

"I know it. Things happened kind of fast Saturday. We obviously didn't think it through."

"Was it a mistake?"

"No." He answered instantaneously.

"Okay. Good." She sounded relieved.

"But I don't ever want you to feel you have to, you know, be with me to keep your job."

"What I did wasn't about job security."

She'd made her point loud and clear—she'd wanted to be with him as much as he'd wanted her. Instead of relief, the realization shivered through him.

"Who's watching Anna?" he asked after another long silence. As if being confused over *their* situation wasn't enough, now he was worrying about Anna, too. He palmed his forehead, realizing how he was thinking like a parent. Was that normal when dating a woman with a kid? Talk about being in over his head!

"Mrs. Jenkins took her today like always."

Oh, right. If Keela wasn't home, Anna would've been there. He couldn't think straight. Though, oddly, he felt better knowing Anna was in good hands.

He palmed his head again. Was that what he wanted in life, to be a step-in father? Because falling for Keela wasn't something he could separate from that fact. And if he wasn't ready to step up, it wouldn't be right to get involved with Keela and keep her dangling while he figured things out. Especially if his answer turned out to be no.

Now that he'd already stepped over the line and slept with her, the least he could do was be considerate. "Anything I can do? Bring you something to eat?"

"I'll be okay." The words were clipped, so unlike her usual melodic style.

Was it because he hadn't made a "morning after"

call? Was she thinking he'd used her and was done? Because that definitely wasn't true. "Uh, hey. I'm sorry if I did anything to upset you Saturday night."

She inhaled and lightly swallowed. "We did get carried away, mostly my fault."

Remembering, he couldn't stop the smile stretching across his face. "That part was great, in my opinion, anyway. What I mean is, my leaving so soon. I was just thinking it might confuse Anna if I was there in the morning." And the thought of spending the night with Keela had felt overwhelming.

The way things had ended with Kathryn—her walking away and never contacting him again—of sensing and eventually knowing he'd wanted and loved her more than she'd ever wanted or loved him, still sent dread through him. He rubbed his temple, where a sharp pain stabbed. Keela wasn't the only one with a headache. His was probably from clenching his jaw so tight.

"It would have been nice if you'd told me that, then."

"Uh. Right. Sorry." She wasn't a mind reader. Truth was he'd learned with Kathryn to keep his thoughts and feelings close to his heart. Now he'd forgotten how to be honest and straightforward, and Keela deserved nothing less.

He listened as she took in another long—exasperated?—breath. "It's okay."

She was ticked off and he was making a bigger mess of things. "No, it's not."

Abby appeared at his door. Horrible timing! "Dr. Delaney, I've got a walk-in from the 4Cs. He says the coach sent him over."

Daniel lifted his finger, asking for a moment. "Ah, Keela, I've got an add-on, so I'm going to have to go."

He felt like a total douche bag using the I've-got-to-run card, even though it was true.

"I understand."

No, she didn't. He should've told her he'd call her later. But he didn't, disappointing himself further, and probably her, for a second time. Why had he thought having sex—amazing sex—with Keela was a good idea?

Because she obviously wanted him, and he'd wanted her for a long time, and…it felt great to be desired. She felt great. They were phenomenal together.

After he hung up and gave Abby instructions to double book the patient, he wondered if Keela had been used to saying "It's okay" and "I understand" with her ex. The thought that he'd just done the same thing put a nasty taste in his mouth, and he left his office feeling as if a brick sat on his chest.

He hadn't saved her faith in men—he'd just hammered another nail in its coffin.

Keela returned to work on Tuesday with renewed fortitude. She'd hold her head high, because she hadn't done anything wrong by being honest, and if Daniel Delaney couldn't see what was in front of him—a good woman like her—she couldn't help him. She'd learned her lesson with Ron.

There he was, looking moony-eyed. "Hey. Welcome back. You feeling better today?"

She couldn't control the sudden flutter in her pulse at seeing him for the first time since having sex with him. "I'm fine, thanks, Daniel. Busy day?"

He gave an exaggerated nod and handed her the schedule. They'd been reduced to small talk, safe and businesslike. She glanced at the list of appointments. Wow, talk about job security. That was, if she didn't blow it by seducing her boss again. Though he had promised what they did outside of work wouldn't affect her job.

"Well, before we start, I promised to give you this." She handed him the specially created thank-you card Anna had made.

He looked genuinely touched as he opened it. Keela scanned her schedule, giving him a chance to study the huge picture Anna had drawn for him at Mrs. Jenkins's yesterday. In crayon and markers, stick figures held hands and walked by a building-sized birthday cake in a field of huge floppy flowers.

He grinned. "This is great. Tell her thank you."

"Tell her yourself," Keela said, heading for her office.

On her sick day, she'd spent a lot of time thinking. Besides her litany of reasons to be attracted to Daniel—considerate, kind, sweet, intuitive, clever with fixing things, a good lover and having the heart of a hero—she couldn't deny what a good father he would be. Maybe if she took a step back, he'd come around and notice what a prize she was, too. Because ready or not, she'd opened up to the man she'd had a secret crush on since day one at the clinic. Anna's surprise birthday had sealed the deal.

When she'd jumped him on her couch, she'd already made her snap decision. That wonderful guy was worth taking a chance on.

She didn't have a clue if she was ready to fall for anyone just yet. At least they had that in common. Both hurt by love. Both hesitant to try it again. But did anyone really know if or when they were ready for the next relationship? She was pretty sure the act of falling for someone new was *never* convenient. The thought of *wanting* to should be a big enough hint.

"Dr. Delaney," Abby said, sticking her head through the reception door. "A coach at the 4Cs is sending over a football player with a dislocated shoulder."

From the hallway, he tossed Keela a wry glance before answering Abby. "He should be going to the local ER, not coming here." Daniel turned to Keela. "Can you get the portable X-ray machine set up in the procedure room in case we need it?"

She jumped into action. "Sure."

"They said the guy got tackled, and now his left shoulder looks out of place and he's in excruciating pain," Abby continued.

"Sounds right," he said, gathering some items from the supply cupboard.

Ten minutes later the assistant coach and the patient showed up, the young, dark-haired athlete grimacing.

"Come in. Nick, we meet again."

"Hey, Doc," Nick said in a guarded manner.

Obviously Daniel knew who he was. Maybe the guy was accident prone?

"How'd this happen?"

"Got hit from behind." The assistant coach spoke up. "He went down and immediately started rolling around."

"Thanks for icing the shoulder and putting his arm in a sling. That's a big help," Daniel said, escorting the teen into the procedure room. Keela was ready to take a couple X-rays but waited for Daniel to examine the patient first.

"Keela, can you bring a chair here, please?"

She brought a straight-backed chair and stepped away.

"Have a seat." He gestured for Nick to sit, and the youth did so gingerly. Then Daniel knelt on one knee in front of him. "Let's take a look at that shoulder," he said, removing the ice pack and undoing the sling.

The left shoulder showed signs of being out of joint, obviously hanging lower than the right.

"This ever happen to you before?"

The kid shook his head vehemently, then groaned and tensed from the movement.

Keela had never watched a closed reduction of the shoulder before but had heard horror stories in her PT tech study courses about how awful and painful they were. Her pulse sped up for the poor unsuspecting patient as she stood behind him, facing Daniel, ready to help out in any way he might need her to—such as preventing the patient from writhing around.

But Daniel didn't look tense; in fact, he looked relaxed and confident. "The sooner we fix this, the less permanent the damage." Daniel had Nick bend his elbow, with the arm close to Nick's body, and put his hand on Daniel's nearby shoulder. Then Daniel rested his wrist on the jock's forearm and began massaging the muscles around the shoulder and upper arm with his other hand.

"I want you to shrug your shoulders for me," he said in a serene voice, still massaging a minute later. He waited. Nick moaned but complied, then Daniel rubbed more.

As he manipulated the muscles, Keela bit her lower lip and held her breath. She was waiting for the dramatic shoulder reduction, imagining Daniel suddenly jumping up and performing some crazy maneuver to spontaneously fix the dislocation.

"Shrug again for me," he said, followed by more massaging and some minor pressing of his wrist on the patient's forearm. And more rubbing of the biceps and scapular areas. "And there you go."

Wait, what? The athlete's shoulder suddenly looked level with the other one. Where was the scream and loud pop she'd anticipated? The crazy jujitsu maneuver?

"That's it?" the kid asked incredulously.

"You're back in place."

"Whoa. How'd you do that?" Nick asked, gingerly shrugging again, to check.

Yeah, how had he done it?

"It's called the Cunningham maneuver. No need for drugs or extra ER time. Just knowing how and where to massage."

Keela made a mental note to look that one up later. On reflex she jumped into action, putting another ice pack on Nick's shoulder and placing the new sling she'd had opened and ready before the patient ever arrived. She looked the teen in the eyes to make sure everything was okay, and he winked at her. Typical jock, all fixed and ready to go.

Daniel invited the assistant coach into the procedure room, then recited a litany of things the patient would need to do over the next few hours, days and weeks to make sure all would be well.

"I'll get the follow-up instructions sheet for him." She started for the supply room. "No X-ray?"

"We probably should. Get an anterior and posterior of the left shoulder just to make sure everything's fine." Daniel rubbed the kid's other shoulder, like an old friend congratulating him. "The bad news is you'll need to wear this sling for several weeks and you'll be on the bench the rest of the summer." He glanced at the coach, then knelt again and gave Nick a truly sympathetic look. "If all goes well, you'll be back in uniform for the first game."

He had Nick's total confidence, and Keela wished she could trust Daniel as easily. But until he was ready to move forward with whatever it was they had, she'd have to hold on to hope.

Seeing how Daniel interacted with the junior college jock once again proved he was good with kids of all ages. Another star for his collar. Keela wished he understood what a natural he was with Anna, too. That was the biggest part of being a parent, knowing how to relate to kids, not treating them like little adults. Kids really were different creatures, and Daniel instinctively knew that.

She'd bet he probably considered what he'd just done for Nick—winning his confidence, keeping him calm—as nothing more than a doctor's bedside manner.

Heat warmed her cheeks at the thought of his bedside manner. Well, he'd certainly proved his talent in that department with her, too. *Inside* the bed.

As the week went on, Keela liked how working together was regimented and safe, if nothing more. They knew this routine well. She got to see Daniel every day and secretly watch him—how he treated his patients, and Abby… How considerate he was of Keela herself, even though he'd dialed everything back to "pre-sex" times. Then she'd go home and process her feelings.

Which were growing, despite her attempts to be cautious. A good man was a good man; it couldn't be denied. And she'd love to explore where that might lead with Daniel. She strongly suspected he didn't do casual relationships, either. Now that she was beginning to understand how she felt about him, what the possibilities might be, it was still up to him to decide whether he could be all in or forever stay her boss.

As she'd realized the other night in bed, after he'd left, it was up to Daniel to figure things out. As for her, she'd been adding daily to her already long list of his good qualities, and she grew more confident every day regarding how she felt about him. Scary as that was.

Thursday noontime, Keela ran late with the postsurgical rotator cuff and shoulder repair rehab class, in part thanks to Mrs. Haverhill's endless questions. Keela finally escorted the group of eight to the door, the older woman hanging back, with concern wrinkling her already wrinkled brows.

"Is it because of my age that I don't seem to be improving as fast as everyone else?"

Keela stopped and smiled as sincerely as she knew how. "Be diligent with the exercises. Don't give up. It's not a competition, it's rehab. *Your* rehab." She gently gripped the lady's unaffected arm. "You're doing great. Honestly." *For a woman your age.*

It seemed to do the trick and Mrs. Haverhill was soon on her way, but not before Keela smelled something delicious coming from the lunchroom. She followed her nose.

As if waiting for her, Daniel popped his head out the door. "Come take a break with us. I've ordered pizza."

Abby was in the middle of taking a huge bite of her slice and looked nearly in heaven.

"We've been keeping crazy hours, and I just wanted to make sure everyone was getting lunch." He handed Keela a can of soda, and she noticed it was the same kind they'd had at her house. The man was also astute. "There's salad, too."

"Thanks. Wow, the pizza smells great."

"I noticed you've been skimping on your lunches this week."

He was watching her, too? "Just trying to keep up with the schedule." Yes, she'd been eating in her office while catching up on her computerized patient-care plans. She accepted the paper plate holding a super huge slice of cheese pizza with a smile. He smiled back and her heart fluttered like hummingbird wings, so she diverted the reaction by adding some salad to the plate.

"There's pepperoni here, too, if you want."

"That's Anna's favorite," she said, just before devouring the tip of her pizza slice. Wow, it was good!

"Take a couple of pieces home for her. Tell her Dr. Dan sent them."

"She'll love that. Thanks. But you should call her." He hadn't yet phoned to thank Anna for the special card she had made for him, and Keela knew how much a call would mean to a little girl in search of a father figure. "She asks about you every day."

He paused, his own slice of pizza half-eaten, and glanced at her thoughtfully. "Tell her I'll be in touch soon, okay?"

Keela nodded, wondering if he was talking in code. Oh, how low she'd slumped because of his inaction, forced to imagine and hope that Daniel would see the light.

She stuffed another huge bite in her mouth and chewed, wishing she didn't care so much.

"You know what? Give me Mrs. Jenkins's number and I'll call her right now."

Had he read her mind? Encouraged, Keela reeled off the phone number.

"Hi, this is Dr. Dan. Is Anna there?" He waited a few seconds. "Hey, squirt! I wanted to tell you how much I love your drawing."

Keela could hear Anna's squeal all the way across the lunchroom table.

"Yes, you did a great job." He paused and listened. "Okay, I'll quit calling you squirt, squirt. Oops."

Keela heard the loud giggles, and it made her smile, too.

"What's that?" He paused again. "Well, how about you call me Oh Danny Boy, then." Another pause. "Okay, then Dr. Dan it is. Listen, squirt, my pizza is getting cold." He glanced at Keela and winked. "Yup, Mom's bringing you some for your dinner. Okay. Talk later, and thanks again for my beautiful picture."

After that, the three of them sat companionably, chowing down on thin-crust pizza and salad with contented smiles, and Keela continued to hope the group meal was a prologue for more. But when they'd all finished, Daniel helped clean up before dashing out to see more patients. She went home that night remembering their shared smile earlier, and deciding that would have to do until the man learned how to seize the day.

On Friday, she finished the week without as much as an offer of an after-work call or an invitation for a kiss, dashing all hope for an actual date. Man, the guy didn't have a clue how to make plans with a woman. Or maybe he simply didn't want to. That hurt. And it took extra energy to hold her head high when she left the clinic for the weekend.

With each passing day, and especially by Friday, Daniel had seen the usual lively glow fade from Keela's eyes. She may as well have socked him in the gut for the way it made him feel. Being paralyzed in the old rut of *love hurts* was a bitch, and he hated being stuck there. Yet he still was. Kathryn had done a number on him, all right.

The college dominated the clinic schedule, and he had regular clients he had to see on top of that, not to mention the occasional emergency. The nonstop pace would continue the rest of the summer, too. Good for work and bad for new relationships. It was just the way it was for now. Or was that a handy excuse?

Every day ended with Daniel exhausted and ready to crash. Yet at night he thought about Keela. About holding her in his arms. Especially remembering that moment when he'd entered her, how good they were together, how receptive and great she'd felt. They'd quickly figured out what turned each other on, and they naturally seemed to belong together. So why was he keeping her at arm's length?

Because it was better this way than making promises he couldn't keep. Imagining disappointment on Anna's face if he didn't follow through—and the more concealed hurt in Keela's eyes—would make him feel like a total heel. He might be annoyingly slow when it came to taking things to a new level with Keela, but better to be annoying than to be an ass like her ex.

Friday night Daniel sat in his office staring at his computer. His father had once taught him a way to help make a decision. The old "fold a piece of paper in two" approach, and writing down the pros and cons of the issue in each column. He forced himself to do it now and was surprised to see the excuses he tried to pass off as reasons to not get involved with Keela. Pathetic.

Was he going to let Kathryn continue to rule and ruin his life? Would the heartbreaking loss of Emma keep him from ever opening his heart to another kid? That revelation assured a long and boring life. Put that way, in writing, his taking the safe route seemed nothing short of cowardly and stupid. And risky, if Keela got fed up waiting and lost interest in him while he dragged his feet. He didn't want to lose her.

He finished up some bookkeeping, wishing things were different. Yes, business was booming—he couldn't be happier about that. But a guy needed balance in his life, and after making his list, he knew who he wanted that balance with. He needed to face the fact that Keela was a wonderful woman and he'd fallen for her. And since she'd managed to pry open his heart again, shouldn't he give whatever it was they had a chance?

Once and for all, Daniel needed to figure out if Anna was a complication or a gift. The way he enjoyed himself around her partly answered his question, a gift, but the strained relationship with her natural father was the part he kept getting hung up on. The guy was unpredictable and could become a huge problem, a definite complication.

Having had enough personal debates for the night, he turned off his computer and packed up, heading out for the Friday football scrimmage at the 4Cs, with his mind as jumbled as ever.

"Where there's a will, there's a way," his grandda always said.

But life never seemed that simple. Daniel needed someone to talk to who didn't believe in fate and selkies and platitudes to solve all life's problems. He needed the man he'd looked up to all his life. His best and favorite mentor. His father.

As he got into his car, he sent a quick text. Going to 4Cs football game. Join me?

Chapter Eight

Keela arrived home Friday night to a blinking light on her answering machine. It was a message from Ron. *Hey, I was away last weekend and obviously I missed Anna's big day. Call me. I want to take her to Disneyland. I'll bring her home Sunday night.*

Away, my arse. Earlier that week she'd posted a couple photos on Facebook of Anna, Daniel and her wearing the silly birthday hats. One with Anna mastering the party blowout, and Daniel right there beside her, grinning, was particularly cute. They'd spent several minutes blowing the party favors into each other's faces to see who could keep from flinching. The memory made her smile, even though she was listening to a lame message from Ron. He probably had seen the photos and this belated trip was more about someone moving in on his territory than making up for a missed birthday. Keela had become cynical since divorcing Ron, but she adjusted her negative thoughts for her daughter's sake. The man wanted to take her somewhere, and Anna had always wanted to go to Disneyland.

After giving herself a stern talking-to, and a reminder not to back down, she returned the call. Since the divorce, she'd been developing her spine. "You realize she's still wearing a cast and probably won't be able to go on a lot of the rides, right? Oh, and you might need to use a wheelchair if she gets tired from walking on crutches around such a big place. You still want to take her?"

"Uh, good point. Maybe next year. Let me talk to her, though."

Yeah, she'd become cynical for a reason. *Thanks, Ron.*

When Anna hung up, she was all excited about "Daddy" taking her out to lunch on Saturday. Keela hoped and prayed he wouldn't let her down yet again. She'd lined up a few more massages for Saturday and wouldn't be around to console Anna if her father stood her up.

Going to bed early with an uneasy feeling, she thought about Daniel wearing that silly hat. How he'd insisted they all have a piece of each birthday cake, which meant double ice cream servings, which tickled her daughter to no end. It was also an obvious and noble attempt not to leave Keela and her humble birthday baking efforts outclassed by the flashier cake.

Remembering the sensitive gesture put a smile on her face, and she fell asleep to pleasant dreams. Daniel was one of the good guys, a Kristoff. Ron was a Hans.

The fatal flaw in Daniel's big plan to watch the football scrimmage together that Friday night was not planning on his dad bringing Grandda. Devoted to his father, Sean Delaney spent as much time as possible with him. Because, as he'd told Daniel many times over the last couple years, who knew how much longer Da would be around.

So Daniel watched the game sitting in a secluded section of bleachers with his father and grandfather and tried not to let on he had something major on his mind.

"Do they sell those corn chips and chili thingies here?" Grandda asked after a few plays. In all his years in the United States, he'd never warmed to football, still preferring soccer, or better yet, rugby. No wonder his mind was wandering.

"You mean Gut Busters? Yeah," Daniel said. "Probably their biggest seller. Didn't it give you indigestion the last time you had one?"

"Well, it all goes for a good cause, right? I can always take an antacid later."

"Da, if you're going to the snack bar, could you bring me a frozen lemonade?" Sean asked.

He gave an assured nod. "Daniel? Bring you anything?"

"I'm good. Thanks." Not really.

Off went Padraig Delaney, using his golf club as a cane, down the bleachers and across the football field with a noticeable jaunt to his step, in search of something to upset his stomach.

Thanks to the warm evening, they sat in short-sleeved shirts high up in the bleachers, a view of the ocean off in the distance. The outside grill overpowered the scent of the sea with greasy hot dogs and hamburgers.

Daniel hoped his physical medicine services wouldn't be needed much tonight, so he could at least enjoy the time with his dad and grandfather. But mostly he hoped to talk to his father.

He'd always looked up to him, not only because he was several inches taller, and Daniel had inherited his height from his mother's side of the family—the only brother who had—but also because Sean was a wise and thoughtful man.

Daniel smiled and scratched the back of his neck. He had something on his mind, and now was his chance. "How did you know Mom was the right woman for you?"

His father gave him a curious glance before taking a few seconds to think. "That was easy. She was genuinely sweet and good—not to mention great looking—and she put up with my stubbornness. Still does. I could trust her. But the biggest reason was we had that special something. I could see it in her eyes and she saw it in mine." He stared toward the ocean for a moment. "And to this day, that spark is still there for both of us."

Yeah, that bordered on TMI, but Daniel had asked, so he couldn't very well plug his ears and sing *la la la*.

"I've never for a second regretted spending my life with your mother."

Though short and to the point, his words said it all. Daniel took out his list and stared at it. Honest. Trustworthy. Supportive. A good listener. Great looking. Easy to be around. She accepted who he was. He hadn't written the next part down but thought deeply about it. making love had never been so hot or easy, and it was only the first time. Imagine what that could grow into?

And that "spark" part his dad had mentioned? Well, Daniel had certainly seen it in Keela's eyes when they'd made love, and again when he'd handed her the pizza yesterday. After he'd talked to Anna on the cell phone,

Keela had given him that look again. Surely she'd seen that spark from him, too. He'd felt a special zing that went haywire the moment their eyes had made contact. Come to think of it, he'd first noticed that look the day they'd gone out to lunch for Chinese food. Had he ever seen it with Kathryn? He couldn't recall.

"What's that?"

"The list." Daniel was suddenly grateful he hadn't written down that last part, about easy lovemaking. Talk about TMI for Dad.

Sean lowered his brows. "That's what I taught you to do when you had a problem. Keela isn't a problem. She's a person."

"But she's bringing up a lot of problems."

"Are you sure you're not thinking about Kathryn?"

Good point, Daniel conceded under his father's scrutiny. All women weren't like Kathryn, who seemed in retrospect to be more complicated than he'd realized.

"Let me see that." With Daniel's okay, Sean put on his half-glasses and took the list, then focused on the Con side. "Divorced with ex-husband issues." He paused briefly, taking the first item under consideration. "Has a daughter. Now, see, I'd move that to the plus side, since it gives insight into not only what kind of mother she is, but person, too. In my opinion, she's great as both."

"Another good point."

"I've made more than one?" Peering above his glasses rims, Sean looked pleased as he took the pen from his shirt pocket and drew an arrow to the Pro column.

"Been hurt by love." He lowered the list and looked at Daniel again. "We all have. It's what builds character. If she lets that keep her from loving again, she's a fool."

Dad sent a not-so-hidden message to him. *Got it.*

Like the retired teacher he was, he drew another arrow from Con to Pro, as if he was grading a paper. "It's a plus, since she's already gotten that out of the way."

"What about the fact she works for me?" Daniel pointed to the next thing on the Con list. "Wouldn't it be a mistake to get involved with her, because if things don't work out, she'll probably leave and I'll lose her on both levels."

"When did you get so negative?" Sean gazed at Daniel as if seeing him in a new and less flattering light. "Kathryn sure did a number on you. Move that to the Pro side, too, because you already know her work ethic. You've had lots of time on the job to get to know the kind of person she is. And who wouldn't want to get involved with a great guy like you?" Spoken like a proud father.

Nothing like a little flattery to build a guy's confidence. Beyond that, Dad was making too much sense. But then, Daniel had hoped he would help clarify things that currently seemed just beyond his own understanding. That was why he'd asked him here tonight.

"So that leaves a very lopsided list," Dad said. "I only see one reason on the Con side—divorced with ex-husband issues. One to, what, a dozen?"

"What're you two yappin' about?" Grandda was back much sooner than Daniel expected.

"Daniel's got lady problems."

"No, I don't." Well, theoretically he did, but did Grandda need to know he did?

"Is this about that lovely lass from Éire? Keela?"

"Yes," Sean answered, since Daniel's jaw was stuck in grind mode. The last person he wanted to know what was going on was his meddling grandfather.

"She's the one, Danny Boy." He popped an extra large corn chip covered in greasy, cheesy chili into his mouth and chewed loudly. "If you love her, you'll find a way around all the little *tings*." Only then did he hand the frozen lemonade to Sean.

More platitudes. *Where there's a will, there's a way.* Blah blah blah…

"So the question is, are you ready for her?" Mr. Smug crunched more, but he'd made his point.

I do have it bad. And cliché comments or not, they'd both helped him make up his mind. "I'll keep you posted."

"Now, don't go jumping into anything just yet," Grandda said, taking Daniel by surprise. What happened to *If you love her, you'll find a way*? Not that he had a clue if he loved her or not, since he'd kept her at arm's length for four months…until he'd hopped into the sack with her last Saturday night. And he'd sure felt something extra special when they'd made love. But he'd been so busy pushing down his feelings for the last year and a half, he'd forgotten what the big *L* felt like.

"Court your lady right. She deserves it," Grandda waxed wisely, waving a corn chip around and dripping chili on his wrist. "Don't go getting all serious right off. Have a little fun." He licked off the chili.

That could be tough with his busy schedule, her working two jobs and having Anna to take care of. "Things are pretty hectic with work and all. For her, too."

"Make time. Where there's a will, there's a way."

And there it was, the mother of all pat solutions. But damn, it was true!

"Dr. Delaney?" A slightly out-of-breath high school

student had just taken the bleacher steps two at a time. "We've got an ankle injury on the sideline."

Daniel stood. If he'd been watching instead of chatting, he would have known that. "Be right there." He gazed at the two men, his mentor and his muse—as in a*mus*ing Irish grandfather—and smiled. "Thanks for your help. I've got some thinking to do, but you've both made great points."

"Go with your gut, son," his father said as Daniel headed down the bleachers.

Losing Kathryn and Emma may have shredded his heart, but his instincts were still intact. They'd been trying to get him to notice Keela for a long time, and now that he had, well, he'd take both Dad's and Grandda's advice.

Later that night he sat on the balcony of the closed hotel restaurant, nursing a beer, thinking and listening to the ocean somewhere out there in the dark.

Conor had just gotten off work and approached, stripped down to his white T-shirt and sheriff uniform slacks. "What's up?"

"Just thinking. Making some plans."

"Aren't you busy enough?"

"These are personal plans."

His "little" brother sat next to him on the creaky bench, looking more like a pro quarterback than a law enforcement officer. "Ah, the complicated stuff."

"You got that right."

They both sat forward, elbows resting on their knees, and stared into the night. Daniel turned the longneck beer bottle around and around.

"You want to talk. I'll listen."

He'd gotten enough advice tonight, but maybe he

could bounce a few ideas off Conor, since he'd offered. "It's about Keela."

"Your sexy employee."

"You think so?" He turned to read his brother's expression.

"Are you blind?"

"No, as a matter of fact I'm not. I don't know how I feel about my *brother* noticing her, though."

He winked. "Go on."

"So Grandda says I need to court her, but that will include Anna, too. I've never courted a mother-daughter combo before."

"Then think à la carte. Focus on the mom. What's between you two has to come first."

He took another drink of beer. "Her self-esteem took a hit during her divorce. I don't want to do anything to make it worse." He was pretty sure he already had by not even attempting to make plans with her since their night in bed. "And I don't want Anna to feel left out." Getting back into dating again seemed daunting enough, but adding the responsibility for Anna gave him pause. What was he supposed to do?

"With my track record of bowing out of engagements," Conor said, "I'm probably not the right guy to give advice, but be sure to let Keela know you care, and don't forget it's the little things that make a difference to a woman. As for Anna, bring her along sometimes, but not all the time. Whatever's going on is between you and Keela."

Daniel finished his beer. The little things. Hmm. That made perfect sense. *Between me and Keela first.* He stood, shook his brother's hand. "Thanks, man. I think I know what I need to do now."

And it started with leaving his past where it belonged. Behind him. Finally. Of course, he'd never ever forget Emma; he thought about her every day, and she'd always hold a special place in his heart. But Kathryn had left him. It was finally time he left her, too.

Saturday afternoon, Keela had finished her massages at The Drumcliffe, had gotten paid and was heading to her car when she saw Daniel pull into the parking lot. He honked and waved, so she waited.

"Hey," he said, jumping out of the car in jeans and a bright blue polo shirt with the 4Cs logo on it. "Going home to Anna?"

"Nope, she's with her dad."

That was surprising. "Got any plans for later?" No time like the present to take advantage of an opportunity.

"Uh, not really. Anna won't be back until tonight."

"In that case, feel like having a late lunch?"

Twenty minutes later, they sat in the Drumcliffe restaurant, eating the fresh catch of the day, mahimahi, the hotel chef's special kale salad, with enough added goodies to subtract the "health food" factor, and steamed red potatoes smothered in melted butter and dill weed. Good solid food, but nothing great enough to put the family hotel on the tourist map. Still, Daniel always liked eating there, especially now with Keela.

"I think it's great how your mother takes Daisy around the hotel so guests can pet her," Keela said in between bites.

"Daisy likes it, too. We've been toying with making the hotel pet friendly, to increase business, but Dad's still weighing the pros and cons." Which made Daniel think about his own list his father had evaluated and blown off as a nonlist. Sitting across from Keela, enjoying the depth of her breezy blue eyes, he was inclined to agree.

She looked great in the black scrubs with Drumcliffe Hotel embroidered on them—his mother's latest bright idea. Her hair was pulled back in a low ponytail, and she smelled like a combination of lavender and rosemary, which she'd probably used to help her clients relax. He glanced at her hands, wondering about their healing touch. He'd certainly felt it when they'd made love.

Great, now the tips of his ears were hot.

He saw movement over her shoulder and couldn't help but notice Grandda stepping into the hotel lobby. Daniel fought the urge to scrunch down below the top of the booth so Grandda wouldn't see them. Too late. Grandda waved, his toothy grin a bit broader than usual. But rather than make a beeline for their table, he had the good sense to take a U-turn and head for the pub. Whew. The old guy was wiser than he looked.

Seeing his grandfather stressed the need for urgency. They'd eaten in the hotel because it was handy and immediate, but at any given time, one of his family members could crash their private party. Daniel needed to move to another venue.

"Since Anna's with her dad, you feel like seeing a movie?"

She worked to conceal her surprise, or was it more of a suspicious expression? "Is this a date?"

He grimaced. "I'm really bad at this, aren't I?"

She reached across the table to squeeze his hand. "You're doing fine. I just never expected—"

"Me to finally get my act together and ask you out?" He tried his charming grin and she laughed good-naturedly. "I know, right? Kind of cart before the horse."

Then she blushed. Hell, they'd already slept together;

it was about time he asked her out. On a real date. Just the two of them.

"I'd like that. But I need to go home and change."

So did he, since they'd intercepted each other in the parking lot, her leaving her new part-time job and him coming back from morning football practice, also wearing a shirt with a logo on it.

After they'd spent the rest of their lunch deciding which movie to see and where, Daniel escorted Keela to her car. "So, I'll pick you up in an hour."

Her bright smile and pinking cheeks gave him confidence he hadn't felt in a long time, and he was glad he'd finally asked Keela out.

Then, riding a high and surprising himself, he kissed her in the parking lot, not caring if every single member of his family saw it. He caressed her jaw and let her know how good she made him feel by kissing her long and sweetly. Mmm, he wanted more, but he had a date to get ready for. When he ended the kiss, she gave him that dreamy look he'd missed all week. Taking her on a date turned out to be the best idea he'd had in a long time.

Three hours later, after enjoying an action adventure movie, they were back at Keela's cottage. Daniel had held her hand during most of the movie, and she'd gotten used to being near him in a nonwork situation. It felt good to dial things back a bit to a regular, everyday kind of date, after the crazy things they'd done the night of Anna's birthday. It also felt freeing not to have Anna there, though she immediately felt guilty thinking it, Anna being stuck with her father for the afternoon and into the evening.

She glanced at her watch; it was almost six. She

hoped to spend whatever time they had left kissing him. Standing in the kitchen, in between her attempts to pour iced tea, he caressed her face and kissed her tenderly. She loved it when he did that, but she worried she might pour the tea on their feet if he kept it up.

Keela's phone rang, and she reluctantly broke off their kiss to answer.

Anna was on the line and she sounded excited. "Can I spend the night at Daddy's?"

"Are you sure?" Since when had Anna wanted to spend more time with her father?

"Yes, I like Diesel and we're going to have pizza for dinner and I get to watch a movie."

They hadn't eaten yet? "That certainly sounds like fun. Okay, then, I'll pick you up in the morning." But she needed an explanation for the change in plans. "Can I speak to your daddy?"

"What's up?" Ron asked, a moment later.

No hello, how are you, just what's up?

"Just wondering about the change in plans. She didn't go prepared to spend the night."

"She'll be fine." Curt, barely tolerating her concerns. What else was new? She prayed he didn't treat Anna that way, but she'd just heard how happy her child was.

"Have you got a toothbrush for her? Something to sleep in?"

"She'll be fine. Quit trying to ruin the fun." He practically snarled, and her stomach knotted. Just like old times.

"I'm not. I'm just being practical."

"Is this because you don't want her staying here?"

"No, of course not. I'm glad you invited her."

"Make sure you're here on time. We have plans tomorrow."

Every single thing about this sleepover felt wrong, but maybe she was being paranoid. Hadn't Anna seemed happy? No way could she fake that.

"Okay. I'll be there by ten tomorrow. Can you put her back on?" The sound of Anna's sweet voice helped her relax. "Be good for your dad, okay? I love you. And call me if you need me."

After clicking off, she looked at Daniel, first fighting anxiety over her daughter with Ron, then trusting he loved her in his own way, and letting go. She studied Daniel's handsome face, how he watched her with pure desire in his eyes. How special that made her feel. Putting things in a different light, she could think of this as a gift of time. With Daniel.

"Apparently, I've got the night off. How about some wine instead of tea?"

A few moments later, with a smile on his face, he reached for his glass and tugged her hand, leading her into the living room. She gladly followed. Taking the lead, he sat and pulled her down. She landed on his lap, her white wine nearly spilling over the rim. He hugged her close and kissed her cheek, until she canted her head for a real kiss. That was more like it. A few seconds later they clinked glasses, said "cheers" and, like adults on a date, drank some wine.

It felt great, too.

He put some music on his phone, then took her into his arms and they danced. Could he be more romantic? The song was slow, and she felt special and sexy when he held her. First, she marveled—when was the last time she'd had an entire night off? Then her thoughts drifted to how she could spend hours dancing like this. She sighed, her cheek resting on his chest as they swayed to a classic love song.

"What was life like where you grew up?"

Surprised by his interest, she trusted that he sincerely wanted to know, then opened up and told him about her childhood, and her life in Ireland. He didn't seem to lose interest, either. Two dances later, they sat on the couch and had more wine and continued to talk freely. No pressure. No time constraints. All so very adult.

As the hours passed, more quickly than she realized, they spent their time sharing parts of their life stories with each other. The good parts. Childhood, high school, college. Both avoiding the tougher times. Her divorce. His broken relationship he'd vaguely referred to.

The wine and music did wonders for loosening their lips, helping Keela get to know him better than she'd ever imagined. Seeing Daniel in a new light, someone she was just beginning to unwrap, yet the person who'd captured her interest more than any other man in a long time. He suddenly leaned in to kiss her again, as if he couldn't breathe another breath unless his lips were on hers…

She welcomed him gazing into his eyes as he cupped her face, letting him know how much she wanted him, too. The moment stopped time. She soaked in how special he was and how hopeful she felt.

"Daniel," she whispered, when he'd ended the kiss and held her tight, loving the warmth of his body. "I didn't exactly give you a chance to decide last time."

She remembered back to how she'd pointed to her bedroom and suggested they take their makeout session from the couch straight to her room. She'd wondered if she'd pressured him, ever since.

"About?"

"Sex."

"I definitely liked your decision."

With her forearms resting on his shoulders, his hands on her hips, she leaned back to look at him, gazing softly, hoping to appear alluring. She smiled with closed lips, then grew serious. "It's up to you this time."

He pulled her hips near his, then delved into her neck with kisses, finding the exact spot that drove her mad. After a deep sigh she entwined her hands around the back of his neck while he grazed his lips over her ear and cheek, then delivered a fierce kiss. And she loved it.

Several seconds later, heated up and raring to go, she stared into his eyes, seeing the flare of desire there, and the unmistakable message that he wanted her as much as she needed him.

"Let's go to bed," he said.

In that instant she refused to let old fallout and second-guessing left over from Ron mess up anything.

Sunday morning, Keela woke up before Daniel. She took a moment to savor the man she'd come to know as a lover, now innocently asleep in her bed. Overnight stubble darkened his chin and cheeks. His thick-lashed lids were peacefully closed, his breathing slow and steady. The expanding emotions he evoked in that yummy but vulnerable state made her sigh. He was a man of his word. Everything he said he'd do, he did. How different from Ron. That quality was the first thing that had attracted her to Daniel, the day he'd hired her.

After quickly ripping each other's clothes off last night, and satisfying the out-of-control fire burning between them, they'd taken their time. He'd proved to be not only considerate but knowledgeable, and making love with him had been like nothing she'd ever experienced before. Was it true some people were best suited for each other? After last night, it certainly seemed like it.

A subtle sensation between her legs made her check the hour. Unfortunately, there wasn't enough time to wake him up the way she wanted, shower and still get to Paso Robles to pick up Anna. If Keela was a minute late, she feared Ron would grill her about it, and how would she explain her reason? *I was having mind-blowing sex with my new guy.*

The thought made her grin. She rolled out of bed and made her way to the bathroom, grabbing her purse from the living room chair and checking her cell phone on the way. There was a missed call from Ron, last night. Uh-oh.

She dialed his number. "Is everything all right?"

"Why didn't you answer your phone?"

I was having mind-blowing sex with my new guy? "It was in my purse. I guess I didn't hear it. Is Anna okay?"

"She had trouble going to sleep and wanted to talk to you."

"Oh, no." Keela's heart pinched at the thought of not being there for her daughter.

"She was okay. We let her stay up and watch some TV with us. I was surprised you weren't right on top of the phone, though."

Uh… "I had a long day and went to bed early." She might get sent straight to purgatory, but no way would she tell him the whole truth! "I'll be there by ten."

"Okay. Hey, Keela?"

"Yes?"

"We had a good time."

Maybe the man was finally coming around on the parental part, or was that only his side of the story? "Great! See you later."

After a brief shower, she set off for the kitchen to scald the pot for some nice strong Irish tea and make toast for a quick breakfast. But knowing Daniel was in the other room, she stretched beyond her usual routine and scrambled eggs. Then just as he ambled into the kitchen, looking half-asleep and gorgeous anyway, she scattered some grated cheese over the top of the eggs.

"Good morning," she said, excited to see him.

"Good morning," he replied, with a morning rasp in his voice and his heavy-lidded eyes looking far too sexy beneath his bed hair. She could definitely get used to seeing him like that. He walked right up to her, put his hands on her hips and tugged her near, then kissed her. The lazy smile he gave afterward was as big a turn-on as his beard stubble.

But she had a daughter to pick up, so she handed him a plate of eggs and toast instead of herself, like she really wanted to, and once he'd sat at the kitchen table, passed him a mug of tea. "Milk?"

"I'm good." His sexy gaze went a step further... *Real good.*

So was she, and they'd done it to each other, and her feelings were right where they deserved to be. Happy. Remembering every part of his body tangled up with hers, she thought maybe she'd dressed too warmly for the day.

Risky as it seemed, she joined him at the table.

After a long draw on his tea, he leveled his gaze at her. "So how do we work this?"

She played it coy. "Us?"

"I think we're starting to get *us* down pretty good," he said with a near cocky smile. "I'm talking about Anna."

Keela inhaled to clear her head. Of course Mr. Considerate would think of Anna, too. "Right. Well, I don't want to confuse her."

"Should we keep things secret?"

"No. We've all spent plenty of time together, and I'd like to keep doing that." She nibbled on her toast, considering their options. "I definitely want to continue—" She nodded meaningfully toward the bedroom.

His hand came to rest on top of hers and squeezed. "Definitely."

Inside, she let out a huge sigh but did her best to play it cool. "Good." After sharing another long and meaningful stare, his eyes setting off all kinds of things zipping and zinging through her body, she finished her toast and gulped her cooled tea. Okay, she was ready for the conversation where they came to an understanding, and said it out loud.

Wait! She looked at her watch. "I've got to leave to pick up Anna!"

He stood, like he needed to clear out, too.

She grabbed her purse. "But take your time here, okay?"

He sat back down. "Thanks. I'll lock up when I leave."

She intended to just give him a quick kiss on the brow, but she somehow wound up on his lap, kissing him, forgetting the time. Finally, with every part of her skin alive and tingling, especially her breasts from the extra attention he'd paid them, she ended the kiss and left her house with a song in her heart and the promise for a beautiful day.

Daniel drank more tea, watching Keela pull out of her parking spot, her hair shining in the sun and a smile on her face. He'd helped put that smile there. They'd figured out some amazing moves together last night, and he'd quickly memorized every part of her sweet body. She'd given every indication she liked everything he'd done, too, and thinking about it only made him want her more.

He went back to the kitchen to finish the eggs and clean up before he went home. Boy, was he going to get a grilling from his brothers for staying out all night. It made him grin. He had a helluva lot to tell, too, but he'd keep all the best parts to himself and play down the rest. Otherwise they'd never let him hear the end of it.

How was a guy supposed to, to use his grandfather's term, court a woman with a daughter? He liked Conor's advice the best. À la carte. First and foremost, it was about him and Keela. Maybe he'd start by having flowers delivered at work tomorrow, and every morning after that. He definitely wanted to see her again in the coming week, though he didn't know when or how just yet. He'd come up with something, that was for sure, because, glancing out the kitchen window, he already missed Keela.

And he wouldn't forget Anna.

Friday night, Daniel sat on the sidelines with the football players at their first preseason game and watched for Keela. After a hectic week where they hadn't worked out a time for a proper date, he'd invited her and Anna to come to the game. A man had to be flexible that way sometimes. He'd arranged for them to sit in the bleachers with the pep squad so Anna could watch all the cheers and acrobatics up close.

His idea to send flowers every day had gone over great, and he and Keela had managed to steal several kisses Monday through Friday at work, even though Abby was getting suspicious. The stolen kisses had proved to be the fire to keep him going when the week quickly got out of control with emergency add-ons and extra duty, and group physicals for the 4Cs junior male and female teams. Bringing Keela and Anna to the game was the best he could do for a date. Keela being Keela, she completely understood.

In place of seeing each other during the week, they'd had several long, late-night phone calls, a promise he'd made and kept. They'd even FaceTimed once or twice—he'd sneaked out of the hotel suite and sat on a lounger on the grass. Seeing Keela sitting on her bed in a nightgown made him want to run right over to her house, but out of respect for his girlfriend, who also happened to be a working mother, he didn't. He liked how things were going and sensed she did, too.

Just before kickoff, Daniel spotted Keela with Anna and waved. The five-year-old jumped up and down and clapped before waving back. He worried she might slip through the opening of the stadium bleachers but knew Keela wouldn't let that happen.

He grabbed one of the players who never made it off the bench for games. "Greg, would you do me a favor and buy two hot chocolates and deliver them to the lady with the child over there?" He pointed out Keela and Anna before handing the guy some money, with extra to keep.

The kid took off, and in no time Daniel noticed Keela lifting her cup, steam rising into the field lights, with a huge smile on her face. Anna was already taking a drink and afterward she waved her thanks, whipped cream in evidence on her upper lip.

At halftime he brought them each a hot dog, hoping his services wouldn't be needed much for the team so he could hang out. Though he'd worked with Keela five days that week, it felt completely different to be with her outside the clinic. Of course, after three days of flowers being delivered, there was no fooling Abby that something was going on between them, but they'd still managed to handle their work routine in a strictly professional fashion. Except for stealing those kisses every now and then. At the moment, sitting next to her, their thighs touching on the bleacher bench, all he could think about was making love to her.

"You're s'posed to lean!" Anna said, breaking into his thoughts. "See? The girls are shouting."

Daniel cleared his head of thoughts of Keela and picked Anna up, sitting her on his knee. With her in his arms, he leaned to the left, then to the right, like the cheerleaders insisted with their multicolored pompoms. Then he stood up and sat right back down.

"Why do they say 'fight fight fight'?"

"It's supposed to make the team play better."

"Why?"

Daniel glanced at Keela, whose eyes were sparkling under the lights. She gave him a don't-look-at-me response, her melodious laugh turning him on nearly as much as sitting beside her. The best part of all was knowing that after the game he'd be going home with her, and eventually Little Miss Why would go to sleep, so they could make love again.

Finally.

Chapter Nine

Three weeks later...

Keela couldn't believe how quickly life had changed. She and Daniel had fallen into a "couple's" routine on every level. They saw each other at work Monday through Friday, had an official date on Saturday night, and after they'd had incredible adult time, he'd sneak off before Anna woke up Sunday morning. Then he'd turn around and come right back with take-out coffee, cocoa for Anna, plus muffins for all, and with plans for some kind of group event for the three of them the rest of the day. He was as dependable in his private life as he was at work, and Keela started to believe in her good choice of men. Never had she expected to trust another man after Ron.

Daniel proved repeatedly to be a man of his word. What a refreshing change from her ex, not having to worry. Trusting. Not to say she'd given her heart to Daniel or anything, but to be honest, she was crazy about the guy.

There was one scary part, though. He made her dream again. About a different kind of life. About the future. Now it was time to trust her judgment. To trust that Daniel was worth risking her heart on.

Monday evening, he'd called and promised Anna a trip to the aquarium, and today, Sunday, they'd taken a long drive to get there. They'd spent hours observing octopuses and squid, marveling over an exhibit featuring the kelp forest, then went back and forth between over- and underwater views of the sea otters' crazy antics in the aquarium's replication of the local bay.

Keela had never seen Anna smile and laugh so much in her life. Every time she watched Daniel explain things, help her daughter be brave or assist with the simple matter of Anna maneuvering around the busy aquarium on crutches, Keela's heart warmed and her thoughts wandered to a secret and special place.

If she could put the feeling into a word, it would be—No, on second thought she wasn't ready to go there. Admitting it would change everything, and she sensed Daniel was nowhere near ready to love again. Yet.

Anna had fallen asleep on the long drive home, and Daniel carried her into the house, where she woke up immediately.

"I'm hungry."

Keela looked at Daniel and shrugged. They'd stopped at a drive-through on their way home and got hamburgers and fries to go.

Daniel used his knuckles to knock on Anna's cast. "Is this hollow? Is that where all the food is going?"

"No!" Anna giggled. "Mom says I'm a growing girl."

He mussed her hair. “You’ll always be a little squirt to me.”

Keela loved how Anna had learned to play along with Daniel’s teasing, because she trusted him, too, especially now when she messed up his hair and said, “You’re Dr. Dan to me.”

He got serious. “Maybe it’s time you dropped the doctor part and just call me Dan?” He glanced at Keela, as if to get her approval about letting Anna call him that. She nodded, loving the subtle significance of the moment. Small steps. Daniel and Anna were growing closer, too.

Hugging the stuffed otter Daniel had bought her at the aquarium, Anna grinned. “I’m going to name him Dan.”

“Wow, you’re naming a toy after me? I’ve finally arrived.”

Anna hugged Daniel. The real one. “Because I love you.”

The room went momentarily silent. Stunned was more like it. Keela could see Daniel struggle with how to respond to such a spontaneous declaration. Where she wasn’t ready to say the word, her daughter had fearlessly exclaimed it. Love! Clearly, it rattled him, and he wasn’t sure what to say or do. It rattled Keela, too.

She thought back to the mistake she’d made the first time they’d been together—*You’ve restored my faith in men*—and how he’d run off, practically kicking and screaming, into the night. If Anna’s innocent outburst made him tense up, Keela could only imagine what her own declaration of you-know-what would do to him. Time. They needed more time as a couple.

After a pause, with a serious and kind expression

on his face, Daniel reached for Anna's shoulder. "You know what, Anna-bug? I love you, too."

He hadn't run away. He'd embraced her love and returned it!

He would never lie about anything as wonderful as that, would he? The moment put a spotlight on not one but two hearts Keela needed to guard. If things didn't work out with Daniel, both she and her daughter would be deeply hurt. She'd get through it—though it wouldn't be easy—but she'd had practice before. The thought of her daughter suffering from a broken heart because of Daniel tore at Keela's motherly instincts.

The room felt heavy with feelings and concerns and declarations of love, and though both Daniel and Anna were smiling and hugging in that feel-good way, Keela was overwhelmed and needed something to keep her busy. She headed for the kitchen. "I'm making sandwiches if you're still hungry."

"Yay!" Anna dropped Daniel in a flash and followed the food train. It proved hunger trumped love in Anna's world, which could be a blessing if things didn't work out. Still, Keela worried about Anna falling for Daniel so easily.

After using the bathroom, Daniel came sauntering into the kitchen, smiling at Keela as if nothing life-altering had just occurred, and the mere sight of him made her insides quiver. He joined Anna at the table.

"You want a sandwich, too?"

"No, I'm good. Just keeping Anna-bug company."

Warmth thumped through Keela's chest. Could the guy be any sweeter? Or sexier? Or more lovable?

Her cell phone rang, and with a heart loaded with good vibes, she answered with a smile in her voice.

If anything could leach the joy from her, Ron could.

Though he sounded in a good mood himself when he asked to speak to Anna. "Sure. She's right here. I'll get her."

Keela handed the phone to Anna, her instincts on alert. "It's your dad." The child went quiet for an instant before taking the device.

Three weeks ago, when she'd stayed overnight at her father's, Anna had told Keela that he'd gotten upset with her for missing her mom, and Anna had cried before he'd let her call. Knowing that made Keela feel guilty. She'd been in bed with Daniel at the time, and oblivious to her cell phone all the way in the living room inside her purse. Anna must have felt abandoned, and it killed Keela to think that. But guilt or no guilt, things had worked out, Ron finally let Anna stay up and watch some TV with him and Ingrid, though Keela shuddered to think what kind of TV that may have been at that hour on a Saturday night.

"Hi," Anna said tentatively, and Keela noted she didn't call him Dad. "Good." After a pause, where Keela could only assume Ron had asked what she'd done today, Anna became animated. "I saw..."

Keela and Daniel grinned at each other as the little girl rattled off almost all the fish, mammals and other sea life they'd seen that day. She really had been paying attention. After another pause, so Ron could talk, Anna blurted, "I went with Mom and my *new dad*."

Keela's soaring heart took the express elevator to her gut, and Daniel visibly winced. The kitchen seemed to have been hit by a shock wave and got stuck in time. She and Daniel stared at each other, her panic reflected in his eyes.

Anna, on the other hand, as if nothing unusual had

just happened, handed the phone to Keela. "Dad wants to talk to you."

Released from her paralyzed state, her rapid pulse climbing up her neck, Keela grabbed the phone, prepared to explain the mistake. But Ron had already started at a sprint. He berated, accused and condemned her.

"She called him Dan, not Dad," Keela insisted to unhearing ears, so she raised her voice. "Ron, I'm not encouraging anything, and you have no right to talk to me like that!"

Daniel went on alert. Anna looked visibly shaken, too, hearing the one-sided argument, her frightened eyes darting from her mother to Daniel and back. No doubt Ron had sounded angry when he'd abruptly told Anna to hand the phone over to her mother, but the unsuspecting kid didn't have a clue. Now she did and she was upset. Beyond upset. Hysterical.

Not knowing what to do, but feeling responsible for the problem, Daniel dropped to one knee and tried to console the child at the kitchen table. She cried on his shoulder, out-of-control sobs, gut wrenching to hear and nearly impossible to take. Like the day she'd fallen in the dunes and broken her leg.

"Daddy's mad at me."

"Now you've made her cry!" Keela yelled at Ron.

Daniel was the cause. His stomach twisted and guilt made him squeeze her tight. Too tight? He'd brought this on. Encouraged it?

The thought freaked him out. If he let himself fall in love with Keela, something he quickly realized he had zero control over, would it always be this way? Never quite breaking into the middle of the family, always kept on the sidelines, with Ron holding Keela hostage over their daughter? Was that what he wanted in a relationship?

Keela wouldn't back down, and he saw the ire she was capable of with her ex.

"You can believe what you want, but I'm not trying to take your daughter away from you. You've been doing a damn fine job of that yourself." Keela hung up. "Eejit!" She paced the kitchen, working off her frustration, running her fingers through her hair, not making eye contact. Anna's cries had wound down to whimpers and shudders as she hawkishly watched her mother.

Daniel rubbed Anna's back when he felt her tremble. He wanted to say everything was okay, but he knew those would be empty words. *Nothing* was okay. A child's innocent slipup had turned into arguments and anger. One phone call had taken their bright day and shrouded it in shadows.

"Daddy hates me." Anna said it as though she'd done the worst thing any kid had ever done in history. It sickened Daniel.

Keela rushed to her daughter and took her in her arms. "No, he doesn't, and you didn't do anything wrong. You just got your words mixed up a little, that's all."

Daniel could tell Anna wasn't the only one trembling. How could one bully wreak such havoc over the phone? Daniel's concern turned to anger. The bastard had probably bullied Keela throughout their marriage. What a horrible way to live.

He made a quick assessment of their relationship from the beginning. Had he ever treated her like that? How about the day he'd told her he wouldn't accept childcare issues as a reason to miss work? *Nice going,*

Delaney. His already twisted stomach tangled into a knot at the thought. He'd bullied Keela as a boss. Could she still be worried she'd lose her job if things didn't work out between them? Could he trust she was as into him as he was her because of it? Or was she only protecting her job? Being with a guy like Ron had probably trained her how to pretend in all kinds of situations.

Daniel hated where his thoughts were going, shifting away from a brokenhearted child to his own doubting universe, but he couldn't stop them. And he couldn't go on blaming Kathryn for all his emotional flaws. He owned this. One phone call. One argument. One tough fifteen minutes, and he was already questioning the very existence of Keela and Daniel. And don't forget Anna.

Keela held her daughter, mindlessly rubbing her back, hoping to soothe her anxiety, as Daniel looked on.

Guilt-ridden and mixed-up, she went over what had just happened. Anna had referred to Daniel as her new dad. It'd come out of nowhere. But Anna had never shown an inkling of worry about the new man coming into their lives. She'd liked Daniel from the start, long before he'd warmed up to or saved her. Ron had been an ogre on the phone, talking down to her. The only reaction he knew for anger was revenge.

Realizing she was clutching Anna maybe a little too tightly, Keela eased up, checked her daughter's eyes for new tears. Daniel handed her a paper towel from the kitchen counter, and she wiped away the trails of water down Anna's cheeks. "You okay, honey?"

By berating Keela, Ron had ensured that Anna's sweet and spontaneous declaration of love for Daniel got stomped on. The message: telling someone you love them is bad. That sick lesson he'd taught Anna just now made Keela's blood boil.

Feeling defeated, she stood and tugged her daughter away from the forgotten sandwich. "Let's get you ready for bed."

As she walked Anna to the bathroom, she half expected Daniel to leave. Wouldn't that be the easy way? Just slink out the front door while the girls were busy. Ron would.

But Daniel wasn't like that. When Anna had calmed down and crawled into bed, instead of never wanting to see Daniel again, since he'd gotten her into trouble, her tender, grudgeless heart was still intact. "I want Dan to read me a story."

It gave Keela hope and made her smile. And it also worried her. "Okay. I'll go ask." She took the few steps down the hall, hoping with all her heart he'd still be there.

And he was.

With a rush of relief, she wanted to run to him, throw her arms around his neck and kiss him. But because of the "incident," and everything it'd dredged up, she didn't. Dealing with Ron had reinforced the old cautionary tale, don't trust men, they change. Ron had poisoned her, and now she worried what could happen, since Anna had innocently declared her love for Daniel. "So, Anna wants you to read her a bedtime story."

"Really?" From the couch, he jumped to his feet.

Keela lifted her shoulders and cocked her head—*who can figure out a kid?* But the truth was, this was another lesson learned from a child who wore her feelings on her sleeve. Only because it was her daughter's wish, she carried through with the request, but inside Keela despaired how easily Anna could get hurt.

He looked honored. Daniel obviously didn't take lightly the reading of a bedtime story to a little girl who'd just told him she loved him and referred to him as her "new dad." Which he wasn't. He was far from it, in fact. They were only dating.

While he read, Keela walked and thought. Her getting her heart broken again, she could deal with, but Anna? The cost was too much and could affect the rest of her daughter's life. Great guy or not, the timing with Daniel was simply too soon, and she needed to think of her daughter before herself.

Fifteen minutes later, when he'd finished reading two books, he reappeared in the living room. Since Keela had had time to think, what she'd decided didn't make her happy.

He stood a few feet away, his bottom lip curled in, teeth planted on top, obviously sensing something was wrong, and he seemed torn about what to say or do.

Earlier, on the drive home they'd exchanged sexy, secret glances multiple times, and she'd been pretty sure they were both on the same page about his staying over a second night. After the wonderful day they'd had, she'd looked forward to getting lost in his sturdy body, letting him take her to that place he'd become an expert at. Now she sighed, wishing things hadn't been ruined by a vitriolic phone call, and all the terrible memories it'd brought up.

But everything had. Changed.

She didn't have the strength to deal with anything else today, so she stood her ground, not uttering an invitation.

"So I should be going?" he said, sounding uncertain.

She'd already emotionally pulled back from Daniel, thanks to Ron, and now she was about to prove it. "That's probably a good idea."

They stared at each other for a few heartbeats, the strained silence taking on the weight of a dozen Rons.

"This wasn't your fault." He took a step closer.

"He acted as if I was a horrible mother for dating someone. Though he'd started dating long before he'd left us. Bloody *eejit*! Who does he think he is, taking the high road?"

"From what you've told me, he obviously did it out of guilt."

"The man is incapable of that." She spit out the words. "He knows no more about guilt or remorse than a pig in an armchair!" She paced, trying to calm down. "I just expected Anna to understand what was going on. How foolish of me."

"We didn't really know what was going on, either. Did we, at first?"

The sweet bubble she'd created around her and Daniel burst, thanks to Ron, and things felt lousy. Really lousy. Too-much-to-deal-with lousy. "Maybe for now we should go easy, make sure Anna doesn't get any more confused." *I'm confused enough for both of us!*

"As long as Ron runs the show, you'll always be confused." He'd poked at an open wound, and rather than admit it, she went the defensive route.

"The man's greedy that way. He doesn't want the job, but he sure as hell doesn't want anyone else taking it." There was no way Daniel could understand their situation. The realization angered her. "I'm so confused. His lousy call has made me wonder where we stand. What we should do." She'd taken another step back from him and was sure he felt it.

"But we're just getting to know each other, though—"

She scratched her forehead, making a huge snap decision before he could finish his sentence. It might hurt less if she came up with the idea. "Maybe we should..." *Should what? Wait until she'd dealt with the fallout from her marriage and divorce once and for all? Or they'd all forgotten the latest incident, when there were sure to be many more?* "Look, I'm going to be brutally honest. Dating you has been great, but tonight proved I'm not ready for a relationship. I thought I might be, but I've still got too many issues holding me back. Ron really did a number on me."

"He's still doing it," Daniel said solemnly, poking more at that wound.

The truth ticked her off. More defensiveness piled on. "You can't possibly know or understand."

He lifted his palm gesturing her to stop, which upset her even more. "Believe me, I have an idea how you feel," he said. "We've both got old junk holding us back. It might be good to take a breather..."

Lost in her thoughts, she got yanked back into the moment by what he'd implied. She'd wanted to start a discussion, test the waters for how deeply he was involved. Now Mr. Considerate jumped right in and said "Let's take a breather." Even though some time apart might be a good idea, it hurt for him to want it so easily. Which proved Daniel was nowhere near ready to love again, either. If he was, he'd fight for her. Did she need him to? God, she really was a mess.

Hurt, anger and frustration formed the perfect storm, and she shut down.

So this was all they had, something that tumbled down on the first test. "Okay," she managed to utter, her insides withering with the sound.

He hesitated, watching her. "I'll see you at work tomorrow?"

Still slightly stunned, and nowhere near ready to deal with practicalities, she answered without thinking. "Of course." After another moment of his trying to make eye contact, and her refusing to cooperate, he turned for the door. Old insecurities piled on to a major truth. "I need my job."

He stopped, glanced back, looking wounded. "I told you from the start that was secure. Nothing's changed in that regard."

He was a man of his word. She already knew it and, just now, he'd proved it yet again. But when he left without kissing her goodbye, she felt empty and her body cold.

Daniel's feet were numb as he walked to his car. How had a great day like today turned into one of the most depressing nights he'd had in a long time? Everything had been going great with Keela since they'd started dating. They'd moved beyond dating quickly and had become involved, seriously involved. Then Ron had barged back in and made sure all three of them had been slapped back into reality. That selfish dude wasn't going anywhere, and he'd always make their lives miserable, if Keela let him, which she still did.

As much as Daniel hated the solution, it was probably good to step back for a while and figure everything out. Both of them. Hadn't he learned a thing since Kathryn? Never walk away from a woman you love.

He stopped midstep. He'd just admitted he loved her. On the night he'd suggested they take a break. Crazy.

He slipped into his car. This wasn't a breakup. It was a breather. That was all he'd let it be, too—just a short break so they could both get their heads straight. There was no way he'd let her go…unless she asked.

In the meantime, Conor had said Daniel needed to honestly admit his feelings for Keela and deal with the idea, then way down the line consider where he stood with Anna, and what he wanted to be to her. For now, she was his friend. Would he ever be ready to be a "new" dad to her?

The whole mess with Ron, but more so how Keela let it control her, made him want to yell. Instead he scrubbed his face, started the car and drove off. He'd take Daisy for a run on the beach, because there was no other way he could work off this kind of confusion.

Keela sat on her bed, finally letting her deepest reaction out. She cried and sobbed, defeated by Ron once again. She'd let Daniel leave, hadn't so much as questioned his decision. Hell, she'd practically led him there! Didn't she think she deserved happiness? She went back and forth between feeling sorry for herself, being angry as hell at Daniel and chiding herself for still giving Ron power in her life.

Daniel had been the best thing for her and Anna, ever. But Anna had called him her "new dad" and that had shaken Keela to the core. Old truths came crashing down. And Daniel had grabbed the excuses she'd given and left, bringing her insecurities back in full force.

Truth was, she had changed on many levels, but this incident had tripped her up tonight. Daniel had seemed to suggest the "breather" too quickly, and that made her want to punch a wall. It was time to give herself some credit, instead of so willingly accept all the blame.

Before they got back together, Daniel would have to first realize who'd changed his life. She'd brought him back from some emotional graveyard he'd been loitering in, and he was in a better place because of her. *If* they got back together, he'd have to understand she was the exact person he needed in his life. Kid and all. With her, there'd be no easy way in…or out. Never again.

She fished around her bedside table for a tissue and blew her nose after wiping her eyes. At least she'd settled something. She was worth it. Worthy of being loved. Then she cried some more, thinking that tomorrow, facing Daniel at work, would be the hardest day of her life.

Chapter Ten

On Monday Keela showed up early at the clinic, hoping to hide in her office before Daniel arrived. Unfortunately, thanks to yet another early-morning add-on, he strolled into the hallway the moment she set foot through the door.

No way could she hide her puffy eyes from crying until she had to change her pillowcase last night. But when she forced a glance his way, he didn't look so great himself—eyes bleary and glassy, as if he'd been awake all night. And had he forgotten to comb his hair? What a mess they both were.

Because it was so hard to face him, she diverted her gaze to her sensible work shoes, the same place the ball of anxiety in her chest had dropped.

But he wouldn't let her get away with avoiding him, grasping her upper arm and squeezing, and rattling her with his touch. "Mornin'," he said while passing by, obviously leaving off the "good" part.

One thing was true: they were in this mess together. So he had the right idea—may as well make the best of it. Or in his case, act like nothing life-altering had happened.

She forced her glance upward. "Hi, Daniel." With her throat dry, she needed water. She also needed something to steady her trembling fingers, and that tight ball of whatever had bounced back from her toes and settled in her stomach, setting off a full-body reaction. "Excuse me," she said, making a beeline for the bathroom.

Once there, hovering over the toilet, she prayed he'd gone directly into the examination room and hadn't lingered in the hall long enough to hear her hurl.

The morning wore on, and gradually Keela felt better. It helped to have her schedule of clients and other duties to focus on. But the knot stayed firmly planted in her stomach, and when lunch rolled around, all she wanted to do was sip tea, close the door to her office, close the blinds and shut out the rest of the world.

Anna had sensed something was still wrong that morning, too. "Are you okay, Mom?" she'd kept asking. Keela had done her best to prove she was, but feeling off balance and headachy, with the accompanying tensed brows, must have betrayed her true feelings.

"I'm fine, honey," she'd flat out lied. "You have a good day with Mrs. Jenkins, okay?" It had killed her to see that uncertain expression on her daughter's face when she'd left her at day care, but Keela had a job to do. And an obligation.

At least Daniel was being his usual gentlemanly self. It had felt good and so normal when he'd touched her arm earlier, though nothing seemed normal between them anymore. The squeeze was probably his way of reassuring her the job was safe, that they'd get through this rocky patch, but the way she felt this morning gave the impression it would be a long road ahead.

Somehow they both limped through the next few days, not exactly avoiding each other, but keeping interactions to the barest minimum while making sure the clinic stayed on schedule. They really were taking a personal time-out. And it felt so wrong.

Something else felt wrong, too.

After nearly a week of having the exact same nausea each morning, feeling queasy and yucky, Keela became concerned. Surely it couldn't all be blamed on her reaction to seeing Daniel. So on Thursday night she looked at her calendar, and icy chills slipped down her spine. She'd missed her period by two weeks! She couldn't very well run off to the drugstore right that instant, leaving Anna asleep in bed, but first thing tomorrow morning, on her way to work, she'd buy a home test to ease her mind.

What else could go wrong?

Friday morning at work—Daniel's day to meet offsite with clients at the 4Cs—Keela almost swooned, seeing the outcome of the home pregnancy test. Right there in the clinic office, where she couldn't exactly let out a scream, because it would alert Abby, she bit her knuckle and forced that brewing shriek back down her throat. Though she had zero control over the tears that slid down her cheeks.

She'd been down this road before with Ron. Turned out, it was the only reason he'd married her. Overwhelmed with defeat, she took this pregnancy as a punishment, not a blessing. She'd been taking birth control pills, too! Except that very first night, the night of Anna's birthday party, she'd been on them less than two weeks. But Daniel had used a condom.

No way did she want a repeat performance with him, when everything had worked out so wrong with her ex. She ignored the tiny voice that said *Daniel's completely different than Ron* and wallowed in her misery a few minutes longer. She shook her head, squeezing out more tears. Why did this have to happen?

Leaning against the bathroom wall, Keela willed herself to recover. She had a group session to lead in ten minutes, and regardless of her personal state, she'd have to be professional. Her life was falling apart, growing more complicated by the day, and now she could think of only one way to deal with the latest setback. Head-on.

Daniel didn't arrive back at the clinic until after lunch on Friday, and the afternoon appointments had them both hopping nonstop. Keela was grateful her morning ickies had subsided long ago, but knowing what she had to do before she left work today put another kind of sickness in her gut.

At ten minutes to five, mustering every last bit of nerve, she marched into Daniel's office. "Can we talk?"

He stopped what he was doing instantly. "Of course." Did he look hopeful?

She was grateful he hadn't said something lame like "What's up?" Both of them knew full well they'd just survived a week from hell, brought on by their messed-up relationship.

"I need to resign," she blurted, without a hint of a lead-in.

He immediately stood, knuckles resting on his desk. "Oh, no, you don't. You need this job."

"Please."

"Nope. Not gonna happen. Whatever you and I need to work out can be done while you're employed."

After their incredibly long, hard week, she didn't have any fight left in her to argue with him. So defeated once again, she turned and left, feeling him watch her until she closed his office door.

What was she supposed to do now?

Saturday was Ron's day with Anna. Since the school year was quickly approaching, he'd promised to take her shopping for clothes, with Ingrid's help, of course. The phone call came at nine, exactly one hour before he was supposed to show up.

He'd canceled on his daughter *again*! So predictable. And Keela was the one who had to face Anna, tell her, then watch her heartbreaking reaction.

Except an odd thing happened this time. Anna didn't seem the least bit upset about it.

"Will you take me shopping, Mom?" It turned out her daughter had more sense than she did.

How could Keela refuse? She didn't have a massage appointment scheduled at The Drumcliffe until three o'clock, so they had plenty of time to buy a few new clothes for Anna's big first day of kindergarten. Just because Anna wasn't upset didn't mean Keela wasn't furious with Ron. She'd finally had enough. The man didn't deserve any power over her anymore. He was a loser when it came to being her husband and Anna's father. What did the Yanks say? *Three strikes and you're out.* He'd struck out months ago, but she'd kept letting him repeat the same stunt over and over, like the comic character who begged Charlie Brown to kick the football, only to pull it away time and time again. Keela may have sunk to that where Ron was concerned, but no more. The man was history.

"Can Dan come with us?"

The question pulled Keela out of her thoughts quicker than a cold bucket of water. "Uh, I don't think he'd enjoy shopping for clothes the way us girls do, honey."

Anna hugged herself and made a pouty face. "Okay, but I miss my Dan."

Keela took a deep breath. She missed her Daniel, too. Though she shuddered to think what he'd do when he found out she was pregnant. She couldn't let herself think about it right then. Anna was very tuned in to her moods, and there was no way she'd give the child a chance to play fifty questions about the sorry state of Keela O'Mara's messed-up love life.

Daniel finished his Saturday morning walk with Daisy over the dunes and headed back to the hotel. Conor hadn't let up on him with questions about his sour mood the past week. Even Mark had noticed that he wasn't spending any evenings at Keela's. Man, he missed her.

Was this what he'd settle for? It may have been Keela's idea to break things off for a while, but she'd flabbergasted him when she'd tried to resign yesterday. Seriously? He'd never pegged her as the overly dramatic type, but her trying to quit a job he knew for a fact she needed sure took things to a different level.

He'd worked up a sweat running with Daisy, and while he showered, he continued to think about the woman he loved. Yup. He'd finally figured that out. He loved her. Seeing her every day without being a part of her personal life had driven the point home. He'd let Kathryn go because he understood, deep down, that things weren't right between them. He'd taken a step back with Keela because he knew they'd get back together—because on every other level, besides Ron, everything *was* right between them. He wanted to be with her, and to be there for Anna, too. All he needed to do was tell her.

Since today was already booked with the 4Cs business, he'd have to wait another day before he made his plea. Theoretically, they couldn't rush into anything permanent, for Anna's sake, but there was no longer a question where Daniel belonged. He was ready to love again and wanted to be the man in Keela's life.

If he needed to stare down Ron and tell him in person to butt out, he'd do it, too. That guy didn't have the first clue how to be a dad to Anna. The main thing Daniel had decided to focus on was the "ex" in Ron's title. Daniel finally had plans to push the guy out of Keela's life for good.

If Ron wanted to see Anna, fine, he wouldn't stop him—as long as it worked with Anna and Keela's schedule. But bothering Keela in any way, shape or form would be off-limits. She'd suffered enough.

The thought of the miserable week they'd had, how obviously upset Keela was each and every day, to the point of trying to resign yesterday, made Daniel queasy. Tomorrow, he'd fix things. He'd make her see how right they were for each other even if he had to get down on his knees to do it.

Grandda's cheeky I-told-you-so grin appeared in his mind's eye, and though it irritated him, Daniel had to give the old guy credit where it was due. Keela was, in fact, the one for him.

Daniel showed up at Keela's door on Sunday morning without calling first, but with coffee, cocoa and muffins.

Anna opened the door. "Momma's sick."

Concern canceled out all the grandiose fantasies he'd had of sweeping Keela into his arms and telling her he loved her. "Where is she?"

"In the bathroom."

He put the goodies on the coffee table, then knelt to Anna's level. "Are you okay, honey? Are you sick, too?"

She shook her head. "Mommy said I can't catch it."

He hugged her close, wanting to make sure Anna didn't worry about her mom. "I'll take care of her."

Solemnly contemplating her waistband, she nodded, worry for her mother more than apparent.

Keela appeared in the hall doorway looking a little disheveled, but not really sick. Surprise brightened her sky-blue eyes, and he realized how much he'd missed looking into them the past week while they'd done their best to avoid each other.

"Hi. What are you doing here?"

"I brought coffee." If she was sick, now wouldn't be the best time to lay his news on her. When he finally told her he loved her, he wanted her full attention, and preferably he wouldn't be holding Anna in his arms at the time. "And I decided one week was all I could manage of taking a break from you," he added. "But I'm sorry you're sick, and if you want me to come back some other time, I'll leave."

Obviously touched by his words, she got misty-eyed. "There's a lot going on right now."

"That's the truth. Where do we start, right?" He wanted to go to her, touch her, hold her, but he sensed her barrier.

She gave a wan smile, which pained him. Why was she so sad? Had he done that to her?

Keela scratched her neck, "Um, while you're here, I may as well ask."

"If it has anything to do with quitting your job, that'll be a no."

She made a better effort at smiling this time. "No, actually, I was wondering if you'd be interested in going with us—"

"Will you be my dad for kindergarten night?"

Though looking surprised at her daughter's breaking in, Keela didn't correct her before completing her sentence. "—tomorrow night, to the introduction to kindergarten."

He knew there had to be more to the story than a casual invitation. She'd probably given it a lot of thought, egged on, of course, by Anna, and it had to involve Ron, who should have been their first choice. Again, now was not the time to ask. Daniel also felt hopeful her invitation was a sign Keela had gotten past their personal issues. So he pulled in his chin to better see Anna. "Are you already starting kindergarten?"

She smiled brightly up at him. "I'm five." There went the hand.

"I know you are. Wow, you're starting school. How exciting." He lifted his gaze to Keela, who watched with a tender but torn expression on her face. "I'm honored you asked." *Please tell me this means all has been worked out.*

A dozen thoughts flew from Daniel to Keela, who seemed to be sending a batch of her own nonverbal communications. That gave him concern. But he was hugging Anna, and dropping the kid for the mother didn't seem like the appropriate thing to do just then.

"Good," she said, leaning against the door frame. "If you don't mind, Daniel, I'd like to rest today."

He jumped to his feet, getting her pointed message. "Oh, yeah, sure. You want me to take Anna for a while so you can nap?"

The little girl went to her mom, holding her leg, and he got the distinct impression she wanted to stay near her when she wasn't feeling well.

"We thought we'd have a quiet day. Anna's going to try on her new school clothes and model everything for me later."

"Sure, I get it. A girls' day. Uh, okay." With her history of an overbearing husband who was now a belligerent ex, Daniel decided not to push back. "So I'll see you at work tomorrow, then?"

Keela nodded, still leaning on the wall.

"If you guys need anything today, just call." He dropped his gaze to Anna. "And I'll see you tomorrow night, squirt." He nodded toward the table. "Don't forget about your cocoa."

Tomorrow, he'd make sure Keela knew of his change of heart, because now that he'd figured things out, it was killing him to keep the secret: *Daniel loves Keela.*

Monday night, after the introduction to kindergarten by Anna's future teacher, they let the children have some playtime. Anna had worn her favorite tutu, which clashed with the neon pink of the full leg cast, but who cared, and had let Keela put her hair in French braids—a first! Miss Juanita had gone out of her way to make the newest batch of students feel safe and welcomed, and Daniel was impressed. Yet Keela still seemed reserved. Not having the chance to be a parent himself, maybe he was missing what a big deal it was to send a kid off to school for the first time. Personally, he was excited for Anna.

Baby Emma came to mind and along with the ongoing heartache of losing her, he embraced the thoughts but gently shut down the memory. Now was not the time or place to be sad.

Keela started a conversation with the teacher, and Daniel stepped back to give them privacy. He glanced across the room at Anna and two little girls, a dark-haired mother looking on. He moved closer, trying really hard to eavesdrop without being obvious. Anna was such a kick and he looked forward to all the crazy things that sometimes came out of her mouth. *Can birds fly upside down? I wish I could drool like your dog.*

The mother of what looked like twins—one with glasses and one with a wide-open expression that brought out his protective tendencies—seemed familiar. It quickly hit him that she was the woman who'd bought the B and B across the street from the hotel, and he'd seen her moving in the last couple weekends. So this harmless-looking lady was the person who'd had his mother in a tizzy about having to compete for business. The three girls giggled over building up some blocks and knocking them over. Apparently Laurel Prescott, the name his mother had been bandying about lately, had young daughters, and Anna liked having new friends.

Keela joined him shortly, and though her demeanor was still a bit distant, he planned to lay everything on the line with her as soon as she put Anna to bed. There was no more time to waste.

"Are you ready to go?" he asked when the young teacher indicated it was time to clean up and say goodbye.

As though she had the weight of the world on her

shoulders, Keela inhaled and dutifully nodded. They walked over to Anna, who was all excited about her friends. Keela introduced herself to Laurel, then made sure the girls said goodbye.

Rather than looking happy and hopeful about Anna soon reaching a new milestone, Keela still seemed preoccupied. Daniel wondered if tonight would be a good time to tell her how he felt or not.

They drove home to the nonstop chatter of Anna animatedly talking about her new classroom and the friends she'd made, Gracie and Claire. But the big adventure had worn her out, and shortly after they arrived, Anna was in her pajamas and ready for bed.

Daniel kissed the top of her head—some of her wild hair had escaped the braids and tickled his chin, making him smile—then Keela led her off to bed. He practiced how he'd break the news. Should he build up to it or lay it right out there? *I love you.*

A short time later, Keela came back into the living room, her brows pulled together, making a fine line above the bridge of her nose. "You should probably sit down before I tell you this."

Ah, crud, was she going to break up with him for good? Not if he could help it. "Maybe you should hear what I have to say first."

That stopped her for a moment. But it seemed her concerns would override his as she took a deep breath, so he blurted out his declaration at the exact time she said, "I'm pregnant."

"I love you—*what?*" Good thing the arm of the couch was nearby. He sat and searched for new words, something to help process what he'd thought he'd just heard. It was imperative he verify before he faced his jagged and still healing feelings on the topic of fatherhood.

He'd gotten to the "love Keela" part and had settled in with the Anna part but hadn't given a thought to making babies! All he could do was repeat, "You're pregnant?"

Keela gave a decisive nod, as serious as he'd ever seen her.

Chapter Eleven

Daniel stared dumbfounded at Keela as he futilely tried to gather his thoughts, simultaneously wondering if she'd heard him when he'd said I love you.

Pregnant. She was pregnant. *Wrap your brain around that!*

Memories of Kathryn breaking the news returned to him, the excitement and hope he'd felt, how that had gotten torn away thread by thread as she kept putting off marrying him. The shock and fear the twenty-week ultrasound results had caused, Emma's congenital heart condition painting a slim-to-none survival rate. How his heart had broken a dozen times over the following days. Her premature birth in Kathryn's bathroom; how he held his minuscule but precious daughter as the paramedic led him, with Kathryn on a gurney, to the ambulance. How he'd had to say goodbye to his beautiful daughter soon after. How he'd never wanted to let her go.

Thoughts flooded his head and old festering feelings forced their way to the surface. His eyes burned, filling with tears. He put a palm with splayed fingers over his chest, but it didn't soothe the pain. Weakened to the marrow, he slid from the arm of the couch onto the seat, dropping his head against the pillow, then covering his eyes.

Keela rushed to him, touching his arm. "Daniel, are you okay? It's not the end of the world." He sensed two more words she'd felt but hadn't said—*is it?*

Up until recently, he would have run off and hurt all by himself, like he always had, but he had Keela now. Whom he loved, and who was pregnant with his baby. Though the fear of losing another child, and not being able to survive it, gutted him. But she was here, right now, and she needed to know why he wasn't jumping for joy. Without looking, afraid he might lose her if he didn't set the record straight, he grabbed her hand and squeezed, then pulled her near.

They held on to each other in silence for a few moments, Keela patiently waiting as he struggled to recover and figure out where to start. Of all times to notice the fresh scent of her hair—the woman he loved. *Tell her. Now.*

He swallowed the thick knot in his throat, then tapped his knuckles over his heart. "I had a daughter once. Her name was Emma." Bit by bit he shared his heart-wrenching story about Kathryn and the baby, laying out every mournful detail. It brought Keela to tears, and he held her as if she was his lifeline. They had each other now. That gave him the strength to continue.

"The first day you asked me to watch Anna, I nearly

fell apart." It had seemed easier to repeat his bitter story with his eyes closed. But now that he'd moved on to the part where Keela and Anna came into his life, he swiped at his tears. For the first time in several minutes, he opened his eyes to see the woman he loved… who was pregnant.

The most amazing expression of empathy was on Keela's face. Of course there would be. Being a mother, she above anyone else could imagine the pain he'd been through. The despair. The anguish that grabbed hold and wouldn't let go. Surely she could understand his loss, and knowing that meant the world to him as he held her near, feeling her cry along with him.

Until now he'd never been able to fully grieve, because everyone and everything focused on Kathryn. He'd had to be brave for her. Take care of her. Let her deal with the loss in her own way, even when it meant leaving him. Then he'd had to pick up the pieces of his life and start over. Alone. A man who'd hoped for a family, had touched it and dreamed of a lifetime, only to have it ripped away.

Then he'd met Keela.

Finally telling her, confessing and sharing his pain, brought relief he'd never thought possible.

"Not a day goes by without my thinking of Emma. Even now."

"Oh, Daniel, I had no idea." She held on to both his hands and looked him squarely in the eye. "How you must have suffered around Anna."

"No. Well, at first yes, but she's helped me in ways I could never have guessed." Of all the odd times to smile… But thinking of the squirt in her pink tutu, Daniel found one tugging at the sides of his mouth. She'd been his kid vaccine, finally giving him immunity. "I should probably let you know I love her, too."

Joy sparkled in Keela's teary eyes. "I'm so grateful, because you know she sure loves you. And I want you to know something I knew long before I got pregnant. *I* love *you*."

They were healing words. She loved him. If that didn't prove she was the one, what would it take? Euphoric, he moved in for a kiss, sensing something he'd never felt before—pure love. He could feel it radiating from her, see it in her eyes. There was no guessing that she loved him as much as he loved her. The knowledge that their love was mutual freed him to finally let go. To give his heart completely. To Keela. And kissing her had never felt more perfect.

But something more needed to be addressed. He pulled away. "You're pregnant?"

She gave her signature bright smile and let out a few notes of her musical laugh. "You okay with that? 'Cuz it bloody freaked me out."

"Ecstatic!" Without a doubt. He squeezed her close. "How far along?"

"Not quite two months. I have an appointment with an OB doctor next week."

"I'm coming!"

"It's during work hours."

"Doesn't matter. I want to go to every appointment with you. This is *our* baby."

He'd set her off again and she cried, those blue eyes glistening like the ocean on a sunny day. Knowing her history with Ron, Daniel understood the significance of him telling her he'd be by her side every step.

Keela's face crumpled with his statement as she buried her head on his shoulder. Yeah, Anna would finally have a father who wouldn't let her down. Daniel would do his best to never let that happen again.

"And we should talk about a wedding."

Daniel and Keela waited to tell his family on the following Sunday night at dinner. It was a gorgeous end-of-summer evening with the promise of a spectacular sunset. But then every day had been incredible since Daniel had confessed his past, and had finally told Keela he loved and wanted to marry her.

In the pub, Grandda sat proudly at one end of the long table and Sean at the other. Conor and Mark were on one side with Mom tucked between them, Keela, Anna and Daniel on the opposite side. The dishes of sweet summer corn on the cob, barbecue chicken, hot potato salad and mixed greens with strawberries were already on the table, creating a symphony of deliciousness. It seemed since Daniel had told Keela he loved her, every one of his senses had heightened. They waited for Grandda's blessing before starting. But Daniel wanted to say something before the wild rumpus of food passing took over.

He stood and used his fork on his water glass to get everyone's attention. Happiness overcame any nerves he may have had about making his announcement. His mother had a particularly hopeful expression after glancing at Keela, then up to him, and his grandfather was already practicing his I-told-you-so grin.

Well, Padraig Delaney didn't know *all* the good news, that was for sure.

"Dinner smells great, so I'll keep this short and sweet. I've asked Keela to marry me."

The table erupted with cheers; even Anna clapped her hands and laughed. Keela broke out in the most beautiful blush, and come to think of it, his cheeks were feeling warm, too.

"I knew it!" Grandda couldn't help himself, staring down Mark, then Conor. "I knew it was a selkie. Do you realize what this means?"

Both brothers studied their plates rather than feed into the old guy's delusions about the day they'd saved that seal.

"This one time maybe you were right, Grandda." Feeling happier than he'd ever been, and supremely magnanimous, Daniel gave credit where it probably wasn't due. Credible or not, the old guy got one thing right. Daniel had finally found someone to love.

"When's the date?" Maureen spoke up.

"Next March." Daniel realized his error instantly, having given the delivery month for the baby, which his family had yet to be told about, and cringed inwardly.

"So you're planning a long engagement, then." Sean broke in, looking as happy and excited as his wife.

"You've got to get married here." Mom had jumped ahead with plans.

Daniel glanced at Keela, still blushing over his accidentally letting the cat out of the bag, and she looked to him to handle the news all by himself. It was *his* family, after all.

He motioned for her to stand, then put his arm around her. "Actually, I messed up. We'd like to elope as soon as possible."

"No!" Grandda led his parents in protest.

"You can't cut your family out of this great event," Dad insisted.

"You want a proper marriage, you have a proper wedding. That's all there is to it." Grandda backed up

Sean, smacking the palm of his hand on the table for emphasis.

Mark and Conor were the only ones sitting back, waiting for the story to unfold. Probably grateful they weren't in the spotlight.

Here goes nothing. "Keela's pregnant."

"They're having a bay-bee," Anna explained, oblivious to the ramifications.

For two heartbeats the table went perfectly still. If it were possible, Keela blushed more.

Then Grandda gasped. Sean clapped his huge hands, and Conor and Mark joined in.

"Baby's due early next April." Keela corrected Daniel's mistake that had gotten his mother's and grandfather's hopes up for a long engagement and big wedding.

"So the sooner we get married, the happier we'll be," Daniel added.

"We're going to be grandparents?" Maureen squealed gleefully, suddenly realizing why they wanted to elope. She looked at Sean. "We're going to be grandparents!"

He laughed, his eyes shining. "Great news, son."

"We'd be happy to have a real wedding here, too," Keela said, "but if you don't mind, I'd rather not look big as a house in my wedding dress."

"How about having it here at Thanksgiving? The coast is beautiful in the fall." Maureen wouldn't let go about them getting married at The Drumcliffe. "And you won't be showing much then. That would give me, I mean us, time to plan the perfect wedding."

Daniel understood where she was going with this. The Drumcliffe Hotel needed to claim its stake in special services; why not add this, too? Well, he didn't want his wedding to wind up being a showcase for Hotel Marriage Packages, that was for sure.

Nor was he about to let his mother or grandfather take over their plans. "Here's the deal. We're having a tiny ceremony next Friday in the judge's chambers at the Sandpiper Beach Courthouse, and we can have a party after that, if you'd like. As for the rest—" he didn't have it in him to break his mother's heart "—well, how about after our baby's born? We could make it a christening and a renewal of vows all in one." He glanced toward Keela to see if she was okay with his spontaneous suggestion.

She happily nodded in agreement. "And my parents could fly over, too."

"Of course!" Maureen chirped through her tears.

Looking into Keela's eyes, the woman he loved like he'd never loved before, Daniel's heart filled with an ocean of feelings that would soon overtake him if he didn't change course. "Now, let's eat."

"Better yet," Padraig said, breaking in, "let's have a toast!"

* * * * *

Don't miss out on the other Delaney brothers' stories!

Mark's story,
SOLDIER, HANDYMAN, FAMILY MAN,
part of the AMERICAN HEROES *miniseries,*
will be available in April 2018.

And Conor's story,
REUNITED WITH THE SHERIFF,
will be available in May 2018 and continue
THE DELANEYS OF SANDPIPER BEACH
miniseries.

COMING NEXT MONTH FROM

HARLEQUIN®

SPECIAL EDITION

Available March 20, 2018

#2611 FORTUNE'S FAMILY SECRETS

The Fortunes of Texas: The Rulebreakers • by Karen Rose Smith

Nash Fortune Tremont is an undercover detective staying at the Bluebonnet Bed and Breakfast. Little does he know, the woman he's been spilling his secrets to has some of her own. When Cassie's secrets come to light, will their budding relationship survive the lies?

#2612 HER MAN ON THREE RIVERS RANCH

Men of the West • by Stella Bagwell

When widow Katherine O'Dell literally runs into rancher Blake Hollister on the sidewalk, she's not looking for love. She and her son have already come second to a man's career, but Blake is determined to make them his family and prove to Katherine that she'll always be first in his heart.

#2613 THE BABY SWITCH!

The Wyoming Multiples • by Melissa Senate

When Liam Mercer, a wealthy single father, and Shelby Ingalls, a struggling single mother, discover their babies were switched at birth, they marry for convenience...and unexpectedly fall in love!

#2614 A KISS, A DANCE & A DIAMOND

The Cedar River Cowboys • by Helen Lacey

Fifteen years ago, Kieran O'Sullivan shattered Nicola Radici's heart and left town. Now he's back—and if her nephews have their way, wedding bells might be in their future!

#2615 FROM BEST FRIEND TO DADDY

Return to Stonerock • by Jules Bennett

After one night of passion leads to pregnancy, best friends Kate McCoy and Gray Gallagher have to navigate their new relationship and the fact that they each want completely different—and conflicting—things out of life.

#2616 SOLDIER, HANDYMAN, FAMILY MAN

American Heroes • by Lynne Marshall

Mark Delaney has been drifting since returning home from the army. When he meets Laurel Prescott, a widow with three children who's faced struggles of her own, he thinks he might have just found the perfect person to make a fresh start with.

Single parents Liam Mercer and Shelby Ingalls just found out their little boys were switched in the hospital six months ago! Will they find a way to stay in the lives of both boys they've come to love?

Read on for a sneak preview of
THE BABY SWITCH!
the first book in the brand-new series
THE WYOMING MULTIPLES
by Melissa Senate, *also known as Meg Maxwell!*

"Are you going to switch the babies back?"

Shelby froze.

Liam felt momentarily sick.

It was the first time anyone had actually asked that question.

"No, ma'am," Liam said. "I have a better idea."

Shelby glanced at him, questions in her eyes.

"Where is my soup!" Kate's mother called again.

"You go ahead, Kate," Shelby said, stepping out onto the porch. "Thanks for talking to us."

Kate nodded and shut the door behind them.

Liam leaned his head back and he started down the porch steps. "I need about ten cups of coffee or a bottle of scotch."

"I thought I might fall over when she asked about switching the babies back," Shelby said, her face pale, her green eyes troubled. She stared at him. "You said you had a better idea. What is it? I sure need to hear it. Because switching the babies is not an option. Right?"

HSEEXP0318

"Damned straight it's not. Never will be. Shane is your son. Alexander is my son. No matter what. Alexander will also become your son and Shane will also become my son as the days pass and all this sinks in."

"I think so, too," she said. "Right now it's like we can't even process that babies we didn't know until Friday are ours biologically. But as we begin to accept it, I'll start to feel a connection to Alexander. Same with you and Shane."

He nodded. "Exactly. Which is why on the way here, I started thinking about a way to ease us into that, to give us both what we need and want."

She tilted her head, waiting.

He thought he had the perfect solution. The only solution.

"I called the lab running the DNA tests and threw a bucket of money at them to expedite the results. On Monday," he continued, "we will officially know for absolute certain that our babies were switched. Of course we're not going to switch them back. I'd sooner cut off my arm."

"Me, too," Shelby said, staring at him. "So what's your plan?"

"The plan is for us to get married."

Shelby's mouth dropped open. "What? We've been living together for a day. Now we're getting married. Legally wed? Till death do us part?"